THE Sisters 8

BOOK 5

MARCIA'S MADNESS

By Lauren Baratz-Logsted
With Greg Logsted & Jackie Logsted

sandpiper

HOUGHTON MIFFLIN HARCOURT
BOSTON • NEW YORK • 2010

SANDPIPER and the SANDPIPER logo are trademarks of
Houghton Mifflin Harcourt Publishing Company.

www.hmhbooks.com

The text of this book is set in Youbee.
Book design by Carol Chu.

Library of Congress Cataloging-in-Publication Data
Baratz-Logsted, Lauren.
Marcia's madness / by Lauren Baratz-Logsted with Greg Logsted and Jackie
Logsted.
p. cm. — (The sisters eight ; bk. 5)
Summary: The Huit octuplets discover Marcia's special power—the ability to
see through things—which helps when their evil neighbor calls Social Services to
report that they are living alone because their parents have not returned
from wherever they disappeared to.
ISBN 978-0-547-33401-1 (hardcover) — ISBN 978-0-547-32864-5 (pbk.)
[1. Sisters—Fiction. 2. Abandoned children—Fiction.]
I. Logsted, Greg. II. Logsted, Jackie. III. Title.
PZ7.B22966Mar 2010
[Fic]—dc22   2009049693

Manufactured in the United States of America
SOFTCOVER DOC 10 9 8 7 6
4500365104
CASEBOUND DOC 10 9 8 7 6 5 4 3 2 1
4500214186

For Sensei George Chaber,
teacher, friend.

Annie   Durinda   Georgia   Jackie

Marcia   Petal   Rebecca   Zinnia

PROLOGUE

Questions! Questions! Questions!

The lives of the Sisters Eight are simply *filled* with questions!

Of course, there are a few things they know the answers to.

They know that each has to discover her individual power and gift in order to figure out what happened to Robert and Lucy Huit, the Eights' model father and scientist mother. They've already discovered the powers and gifts for four Eights. Annie has the power to be as smart as an adult when needed, and her gift is a ring with a purple gemstone. Durinda's power is that if she pats her right leg three times rapidly and then sharply points her finger at someone, she can freeze a person for various lengths of time (except it doesn't work for Zinnia). Durinda's gift is dangly screw-on earrings with emerald-colored gemstones. Georgia's power is that she can twitch her nose twice and make herself invisible. Her gift, which she initially sent back, is a gold compact mirror with her name engraved on the front. Jackie's power is that she can run faster than a speeding train. Her gift is a red cape—*not* monogrammed like Superman's.

What will the powers and gifts turn out to be for the remaining Eights?

Nobody knows yet.

Some other things they know? Which people are in on their secret. These people include Pete the mechanic and Mrs. Pete; Will Simms, their classmate, whom they love; Mandy Stenko, their classmate, whom they're learning to like more than they once did; and their teacher, Mrs. McGillicuddy, also known as the McG, who was recently appointed principal of the Whistle Stop, where the Eights are in third grade. Well, the McG *sort of* knows. She doesn't want to know everything.

The Eights also know they live in a magnificent stone house, practically a mansion. The address: 888 Middle Way. Country: unknown.

Oh, and they also know they have eight gray-and-white puffball cats: Anthrax, Dandruff, Greatorex, Jaguar, Minx, Precious, Rambunctious, and Zither. How could they possibly forget the cats? But . . .

Questions! Questions! Questions!

At the end of *Annie's Adventures,* they thought Mommy was working on the secret of eternal life, but the Top Secret folder was empty. Perhaps Mommy was trying to throw evil people, like their toadstool of a neighbor the Wicket, off track? So they're not really sure what's going on with that.

At the end of *Durinda's Dangers,* having sent the Wicket on a wild-goose chase to Beijing, they began wondering if there might be other enemies out there in the world. This has been partially answered. Serena Harkness, Frank Freud (who was the principal of the Whistle Stop before the Eights forced him into early retirement in Australia and the McG took over his job)—neither of them turned out to be very nice, and there are probably still more not-very-nice people out there.

At the end of *Georgia's Greatness,* they discovered that evil substitute teacher Serena Harkness's real last name was—wait for it!—*Smith,* the exact same last name their mother had before she got married. Is Serena, who looks similar to Lucy Huit but about ten years younger, some sort of relation? And what of that other woman they saw in the picture with Serena and their mother, the woman who looks *exactly* like their mother?

At the end of *Jackie's Jokes,* the Wicket returned from Beijing. What will this evil neighbor do now? Also at the end of *Jackie's Jokes,* a flock of carrier pigeons delivered a ton of scroll-like notes, each with the same message: *Beware the other Eights!* There was a similar note found earlier behind the loose stone in the drawing room, where the Eights always find mysterious unsigned notes. This led to the biggest question of all. As Jackie put it so well: *Other* Eights? *What* other Eights?

Oh, and have you noticed that a book is talking to you again? There's a good question for you: *Who am I?*

Questions! Questions! Questions!

And hardly an answer in sight.

It's a good thing for all involved, then, that Marcia's month is about to start. You remember Marcia, don't you?

Marcia, the sane one.

Marcia, the rational one.

Marcia, the observant one with the scientific mind— you know, the one who would *never* do anything crazy.

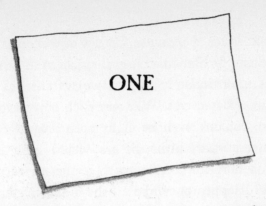

ONE

We each thought it would be nice to be a great detective, like Nancy Drew. If we were all like Nancy Drew, every time a mystery arose we could devote all our energies to solving it. Of course, we'd done our research. We'd gone to the library and looked at the Nancy Drew books there.

That's when we discovered that there were fifty-six books in the original series and that Nancy was eighteen years old in book one and still eighteen at the end of book fifty-six. Marcia had pulled out her calculator and done the math: Nancy Drew solved mysteries at the rate of one every 6.5178571 days. We couldn't compete with that!

We'd learned the hard way that there was no hurrying time. Things would happen *when* they happened, and there was no use in our trying to solve things quicker. We would get our powers and gifts when the time came, and we'd learn answers when the time came.

We'd had to learn patience, not an easy thing to learn, particularly for Rebecca. And Georgia. And Zinnia.

Plus, unfortunately for us, we weren't old enough to be great detectives. We were each only seven years old and wouldn't even be eight until August 8, 2008. This meant that, although we would have liked to spend all our time trying to solve the mystery of our parents' disappearance and all the other mysteries that had arisen since then—like, what was Mommy really working on? how was Crazy Serena related to us? what was the Wicket up to now that she was back? and, oh yeah, *what other Eights?*—we simply couldn't. We had no time to solve the mini mystery of what those two women were doing in that picture with Mommy, and we had no information on other Eights. And no one else lived a life like we did, so who could we ask? It wasn't exactly like we could go to the police . . .

We were too busy leading the lives of normal kids: doing homework, taking care of the house—cleaning up after that flock of pigeons had been no small feat!—plus preparing all our own food, paying bills, driving cars, and fighting against evil when it reared its ugly head. So we really didn't have endless amounts of time to spend on trying to solve the mysteries of the universe, much as we might have liked to.

Yes, sometimes it was hard being us.

* * * * * * * *

"Mayday! Mayday!" Annie cried, emerging from Daddy's study.

"Yes." Georgia yawned. "We all know it's the first of May, also known as May Day."

"Don't you remember?" Rebecca sneered at Annie. "We were all there at school today when the McG, following Mandy Stenko's suggestion, had us all dance around that silly Maypole in honor of the day."

"I thought it was kind of fun," Petal said quietly. "All those pretty colored ribbons wrapping around the pole."

"Ribbons," Zinnia said wistfully. "Ribbons always remind me of presents. It would be nice if it were a real holiday—you know, a present-giving one—so that maybe I could—"

"I didn't say *May Day!*" Annie was exasperated. "I said *mayday!*"

We all reflected on this, at least the ones of us who were there. No one had seen Marcia since we'd come home from school.

"May Day? Mayday?" Rebecca shrugged. "I fail to see the difference."

Jackie looked at Annie. "Do you mean *mayday* as in 'an international radiotelephone signal word used as a distress call'?"

Jackie was big on vocabulary. Sometimes it seemed to us that she had swallowed a whole dictionary!

"Is Jackie right?" Durinda asked Annie soothingly. Durinda was big on soothing. "Is that what you mean?"

"Oh no!" Petal said. "Not a distress call! Does this mean we're on the *Titanic*? Do we need to send out an SOS?"

"No, we're not on the *Titanic*," Annie said. "But we may need to send out an SOS if I don't find out what happened to all those bills."

"What do you mean," Rebecca demanded, " 'what happened to all those bills'? If you're talking about the bills that come to the house each month—for electricity and cable TV and things like that—it's your job to pay them."

"Yes, I do know that," Annie said irritably. "The problem is, I can't find them!"

"I still don't understand," Georgia said, "and that's really saying something. After all, as everyone knows, ever since getting my power and having my own month, I am marginally smarter than I used to be."

"Believe me"—Rebecca held her thumb and forefinger about one-sixteenth of an inch apart as she sneered at Georgia—"that is a very small margin."

Annie shook her head, ignoring the squabbles of siblings.

"It's like this," Annie said. "Every time we get the mail, I take all the bills out and put them in the top drawer of the desk in Daddy's study."

"Oh, that sounds like a real system." Rebecca rolled her eyes.

Annie continued ignoring Rebecca.

"Then," Annie went on, "I pay all the bills on the first of the month. It's a habit I've gotten into since reading a book on household finances that suggested doing it this way so it's easy to remember."

"Well, yes," Rebecca admitted. "You may have something there—you know, regarding a system."

"The problem is," Annie said, "that today is the first of the month, and when I went to look in the top drawer just now—all the bills were gone!"

"Oh no! Oh no!" Petal cried. "This is awful!" Petal stopped looking distressed long enough to look puzzled. "What does that mean, the bills are gone?"

"They're gone means they're gone!" Annie said, looking almost as distressed as Petal had a moment before. "Somehow they've become misplaced. And if I don't find them, if I don't pay each and every bill on time, the bill collectors will come after us."

"Oh," Durinda said soothingly, "I'm sure it can't be as awful as all that."

"But it is," Annie insisted. "It's what that book I read on household finances said: if people don't pay their bills on time, the bill collectors come after them!"

"Why don't we just start looking, then?" Jackie suggested in a reasonable tone of voice. "I'm sure if we all look, we're bound to find them."

"That's good." Annie visibly fought to gain control of her panic. "That sounds like a good idea."

"Great," Jackie said, and then she began to organize all of us. All of us except for Marcia, that is, who still hadn't shown her face. "Durinda," Jackie said, "you search the kitchen."

"What would bills be doing in the kitchen?" Rebecca said with a sneer. "They can't just walk there on their own."

"I don't know," Jackie said. "Maybe robot Betty was using them as a fan to flirt with Carl the talking refrigerator."

"Aye, aye!" Durinda saluted Jackie smartly.

"Georgia, Rebecca, Zinnia, you check out Spring, Summer, and Fall," Jackie directed, naming three of the four seasonal rooms that our scientist-inventor mother had created so we could go to whatever season we wanted whenever we were in the mood for a change. "I'll take Winter."

"What about me?" Petal asked.

"Why don't you check out the basement and the tower room?" Jackie suggested.

"The basement and the tower room?" Petal gulped.

"All by myself? But that's where the spiders are most likely to—"

"How stupid of me." Jackie cut Petal off midworry. "What was I thinking? Of course you can't do that."

"Then what can I do?" Petal asked.

Jackie placed her hand on Petal's shoulder as though she were about to give her the most challenging mission of all. "You just stay here and worry," Jackie said solemnly. "Have fun with it."

"And me?" Annie asked.

"Go through the other drawers in Daddy's study," Jackie said.

And we were off—all of us except Marcia—to do the things Jackie had directed us to. Petal was particularly good at her part.

But after searching all the places Jackie had suggested, along with several that she hadn't, we met up again—all except Marcia—in the drawing room to admit that none of us had had any luck.

"They must be here somewhere." Jackie tapped her lip thoughtfully, and then her eyes lit up. "I know! What about behind that loose stone where we always find the notes?"

Jackie had made it halfway across the room when Marcia sauntered in, hands behind her back, Minx sauntering right along beside her.

Zinnia cocked her head to one side. "Is that Minx I

hear," she wondered aloud, "whistling a tune to make others think she's innocent when in reality she's up to no good?"

We rolled our eyes. That Zinnia! Still pretending she could communicate with cats! It was as though she thought she was Dr. Dolittle!

"What have you been up to?" Rebecca narrowed her eyes at Marcia. "I know what being up to no good looks like because I've looked that way before."

"Rebecca's right," Georgia said. "We've both been there. We've both done that."

Marcia sauntered right up to Annie, produced a fistful of stamped envelopes from behind her back, waved them under Annie's nose, and said sweetly, "Were you by any chance looking for these?"

"The bills!" Annie grabbed the envelopes from Marcia's hand. "You found the bills!" Annie looked relieved, but as she thumbed through the stack, concern came over her face.

"But I don't understand," she said, holding up an envelope. "The address of the electric company is showing through the window on this when it should be our address I see."

"Oh. That." Marcia studied her fingernails as though she'd just had a manicure.

"Yes," Annie said. "That."

"Well, see," Marcia said, still studying her nails, "I went into Mommy and Daddy's bedroom after we got home from school and grabbed the strongbox. Then I got out the black ledger—you know, the one with the checkbook inside." Marcia shrugged. "And then I just went to Daddy's study and paid all the bills."

Seven of us gasped.

"You did *what?*" Annie was practically purple with rage. Purple was a good color for Annie—which was probably why the ring she'd received as a gift had a purple gemstone in it—but not when it was the color of her skin.

"But Annie pays the bills." Durinda was stunned. "She's the only one who knows how."

"I feel faint," Petal said, fanning her face with her hand like crazy. "This is chaos!"

"It's not *chaos*," Marcia said. "It's simple math."

"You probably did it all wrong," Annie said.

"Oh no!" Petal cried. "If Marcia did everything all wrong, Bill Collector will surely come!"

Petal was so upset, Durinda, Georgia, Rebecca, and

Zinnia all had to fan her to keep her from fainting. Rebecca did so only reluctantly.

"I really hate giving in to this panic nonsense," Rebecca said, "but the cats are all underfoot now, and it would be awful if Petal crashed to the floor and crushed Rambunctious."

"Fine." Marcia placed her hands on her hips as she addressed Annie. "Then why don't you check?"

So Annie did. She slit open envelope after envelope, looking to see if Marcia had done everything correctly.

"Huh," Annie said when she was finished. "You did everything right."

"I told you," Marcia said.

"And the checkbook?" Annie said. "You balanced that correctly too?"

"Yes," Marcia said. "But you can go see for yourself if you don't believe me," she challenged.

"No, that's all right." Annie spoke slowly, as though she were trying to wrap her mind around a new idea. "I believe you."

Then Annie directed Georgia to stop fanning Petal and go get the tape so she could seal all the envelopes back up.

"Um, Marcia?" Annie asked after Georgia returned with the tape. "What I don't understand is, why did you do all this? Why did you take it upon yourself to pay the bills this month?"

There was something odd about Marcia's expression then. Was it sympathy? Was it resentment? Was it a too-sweet something we couldn't name? It was a puzzle.

"I just thought you'd be pleased," Marcia said. "I figured it must get tiring for you, being the only one of us who can do certain things. And it really was easy— the bill-paying, that is—not at all like rocket science, which, I might add, I can also do." Pause. "Can *you?*"

We all thought about that: the idea that one of us could do something that previously only Annie had been able to do and might even be able to do some things Annie couldn't, like rocket science.

It was a lot to digest.

Then:

"Durinda?" Marcia asked. "Do you think you might make me a pot of coffee? After all that bill-paying, I could really use a cup of joe."

Petal gasped. "But Annie's the only one of us who can drink coffee!"

And then Petal really did faint.

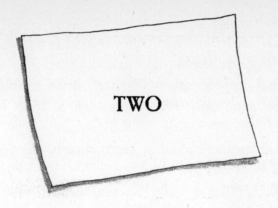

TWO

The rest of Thursday passed pretty much as any Thursday normally would. We did our homework, ate dinner, played, watched a little TV, tried to solve some of the mysteries in our world—failed on that one—and brushed our teeth and went to bed. The only change was that Annie seemed a little more subdued than usual.

But then Friday came, and there was a big change.

When we arrived at our third-grade classroom at the Whistle Stop, Mandy Stenko and Will Simms were there, but the McG wasn't waiting for us at her usual post behind her desk. This was strange, because ever since the day early on in the school year when Jackie had managed to sneak a toad into her desk drawer, the McG had made it a point to arrive before we Eights did. In fact, the only time since then that she hadn't arrived ahead of us was when she'd been abducted. Principal Freud had later introduced us to our substitute, who was then calling herself Serena Harkness.

"You don't think the McG's been abducted again, do you?" Durinda wondered aloud.

"That hardly makes sense," Annie said. "Pete the mechanic ran Crazy Serena out of town back in March."

"Perhaps there could be another substitute teacher?" Zinnia suggested.

"Oh no!" Petal said. "Not another evil substitute! Quick, everybody, hide under your desk!"

"Get out from under that desk, Petal," Rebecca directed sternly. "Don't you know anything? Not all substitutes are evil. And saying that they are would be like saying that all Eights are like me because I am the way I am."

"I'm pretty sure that in the wider world," Jackie said gently to Petal, getting down on the floor to speak to her under the desk, "every time a teacher is a little bit late, it doesn't mean she's been abducted by evildoers."

"Yes," Marcia agreed. "Sometimes there's just a lot of traffic."

"I don't care about any of this," Georgia said. "I'm bored."

"Don't say that!" Annie pointed an accusing finger at Georgia. "Everything in our lives is your fault."

"My fault?" Georgia was clearly both horrified and a little excited at the idea.

"Yes, your fault," Annie said. "Back on New Year's Eve, *you* were the one who complained that you were bored. And it was after *that* that Mommy and Daddy disappeared and all our troubles started."

"That's not fair," Marcia observed. "Saying that Georgia somehow made those things happen makes as little sense as Petal thinking all substitutes are evil or, as Rebecca said, people thinking that all Eights are like Rebecca simply because she is the way she is."

"I don't like it when you all fight," Mandy Stenko said with a shudder. "It's worse than when my parents fight."

"Perhaps we should do something to take our minds off things until our teacher or some other adult arrives?" Will suggested helpfully.

We all beamed at Will, even Mandy Stenko. But that wasn't surprising. When it came to Will Simms, what was there not to beam at?

"Perhaps," Mandy offered, "we could quiz each other on math to pass the time?"

Rebecca snorted so loudly, she might as well have been a horse. "Oh, that sounds like tons of fun, a real ride on the carousel. Maybe after we're done quizzing each other on math, we can each tear out our own fingernails one by one."

"I know what we could do!" Georgia said.

She was so excited, we all turned to look at her, hopeful expressions on our faces. Even Petal, still under the desk, looked perkier.

"We could have another spitball fight!" Georgia said.

Seven Eights, plus Mandy and Will, groaned.

"What's wrong with that?" Georgia looked hurt. "It was fun the last time. Well, at least until Serena Harkness walked in and I beaned her with a big one square in the forehead."

"Your shining hour," Rebecca said.

"It's just that we did that already," Durinda said gently.

"Durinda's right," Jackie said with an apologetic shrug. "We really don't like to repeat ourselves once we've done a thing, not unless there's a good reason to."

"*Petal Huit!* What *are* you doing under that desk?"

Who said that?

Those of us who were sitting jumped slightly in our chairs. Those of us who were standing straightened our postures. Even Petal jolted up a little, banging her head on the underside of the desk.

We swiveled our heads to where the voice had come from.

Oh! The McG! Of course!

Only she wasn't alone.

Standing beside her was a tall man, even taller than her tallness! Where the McG was very thin and tidily dressed, the man was lanky, his baggy gray suit fitting him like a sack. Where the McG had a long nose that she used to hold up her horn-rimmed glasses, the man had a ridiculously small nose—we wondered how he could even breathe through such a tiny thing—and no glasses at all covering his gray eyes. And where the McG had her blond hair pulled up into a tight bun, the man had his long blond hair pulled into a loose ponytail.

Idly we wondered if this last item would bother Rebecca, since she was the only Eight who wore her hair in a ponytail and we'd always imagined she was rather proud of her unique look.

"Who's the dude?" Rebecca wanted to know.

The McG ignored her.

"Principal McGillicuddy," Mandy Stenko said, her eyes flitting back and forth between the McG and the long list of items on the right-hand side of the chalkboard, "yesterday when you made out the schedule for today, you didn't put anything on it about there being a visitor."

Mandy Stenko didn't like unscheduled changes to the schedule. They made her nervous.

The McG had ignored Rebecca, and she ignored Mandy Stenko too. Well, who could really blame her in either case?

"Mandy, Will, and . . . *the rest of you*," the McG announced, "I am pleased to inform you that the Whistle Stop has finally hired a new permanent teacher for your class."

Wait a second. What was this? With it already being May and with the end of the school year next month, we'd been kind of secretly hoping that we could simply finish out the year with the McG. It wasn't that we were so all-fired crazy happy about having her as a teacher, but at least we were used to her.

And maybe we were more than used to her. Maybe we even liked her, seeing as how we had—through Annie—arranged for her to become principal in the first place. And there had already been so many changes in our world this year.

"Allow me to introduce you to your new permanent teacher," the McG said, gesturing toward the man as though he were some sort of prize. "Please say hello to Mr. McGillicuddy."

Mr. Mc—?

"Is he your father?" Petal asked, finally coming out from under the desk. "You do have the same last name, you know."

"No, he's not my *father!*" The McG was clearly exasperated by the idea. "Can't you see he's around my age, maybe just a little older or younger?"

"Is he your brother, then?" Zinnia asked. "I've always thought it would be nice to have a brother. On birthdays and holidays, I imagine brothers give different presents than sisters do."

"No, he's not my *brother!*" the McG said. "He's my—"

"Distant cousin?" Durinda said.

"Young uncle?" Jackie said.

"Old son?" Rebecca said.

"Relative you never knew you had?" Marcia said. "Because if that's the case, we do know what that's like. We have at least one of those, possibly more."

"He's none of those things!" the McG practically shouted. "He's my *husband!*"

Husband?

We reeled in horror at the thought. We weren't even sure why we were so horrified. We only knew that we were.

"Your *husband?*" Georgia said. Then she spoke aloud the thoughts we were all having, at least us Eights. "But if he's your husband, why didn't he come looking for you the time Crazy Serena teachernapped you and held you hostage for two weeks?"

"I'm sure he did try very hard—" the McG started, but then she shook her head violently and glared at us as though this were somehow our fault, like we'd somehow made her answer questions she didn't want to think about.

"Never mind all that now," the McG said. "Mr. McGillicuddy is your new permanent teacher."

Mandy Stenko timidly raised her hand for permission to speak, even though the rest of us were speaking without raising our hands.

"Yes, Mandy?" the McG said. "I'm sure you have something sensible to say about all this. Or at least I doubt you have anything to say that's idiotic."

"But ... but ... but," Mandy Stenko stammered, "isn't hiring your own husband to replace you a case of gross and criminal nepotism?"

"What's nepotism?" Petal whispered to Jackie, giving her a little poke in the side.

"Nepotism," Jackie whispered back, "is favoritism, as in appointment to a job based on kinship. It means hiring someone because they're related to you."

"I believe there are actual laws against it," Marcia whispered.

"Hmm," Rebecca whispered darkly, "I rather like the sound of this nepotism thing. I know *I'd* like to get ahead in life based on something other than merit."

We may have been making the effort to whisper, but everyone in the room could hear every word we said.

"It is *not* nepotism!" Now the McG really was shouting. "Mr. McGillicuddy was simply the most qualified person to apply for the job! Besides," she added, taking the time to glare at each of us in turn: Annie, Durinda, Georgia, Jackie, Marcia, Petal, Rebecca, and Zinnia. Funny, we thought, she didn't glare at either Will Simms or Mandy Stenko. "Besides," the McG repeated, "when the other applicants learned about you *Eights*, no one else wanted the job!"

Ooh! Harsh!

The McG regained control of herself, straightening her glasses and skirt.

"Now then," she said calmly. "I'm sure Mr. McGillicuddy and all of you will get along fine for the rest of the school year, particularly since there's not much more than a month left." She gave a little nervous laugh. "What can go wrong in such a short period of time?"

We stared back at her. We all knew how much could go wrong in a short period of time.

"As for me," the McG went on, ignoring our meaningful stares, "now I can finally assume my principalship duties in full."

And she was gone.

We were fairly certain that there was no such word in the English language as *principalship*. We would have liked to ask Jackie just to be sure, but there wasn't time for that now. We also thought it odd to hear the McG referring to her husband as Mr. McGillicuddy—we had never heard our mother call our father Mr. Huit in our lives!—but there wasn't time to think about that either.

Because our new teacher, whom we already thought of as the *Mr. McG*, was staring at us like we were ten lions in a cage and he was a lion tamer with a chair and whip, while we were staring back at him like *Oh yeah? Do you really think you can tame us?*

It was going to be an interesting rest of the year.

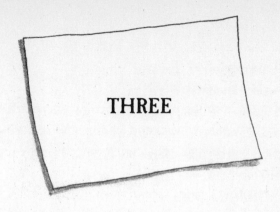

THREE

We arrived home that day feeling dejected. It didn't help that as we walked up the long driveway to our house, we saw our evil neighbor the Wicket staring out at us from behind her cracked-open front door.

As soon as she saw us seeing her, her head disappeared and she slammed the door shut.

"Do you think she blames us," Georgia said, "for her going on that wild-goose chase to Beijing?"

"Well," Rebecca said, "the fake note from Mommy we made for the Wicket to see did say specifically *not* to look for her in Beijing, so if the Wicket is upset about the wild-goose chase, she can't blame anybody but herself!"

"Do you think she's planning to sneak into our house again?" Petal worried aloud.

"I have no idea what goes on inside the minds of evil people," Annie said, "although Rebecca might. All

I know is, whatever the Wicket is up to, it can't be anything good."

We entered our house.

Normally, coming home on a Friday was our happiest time of the week, a weekend of fun and leisure—or as much as we ever had, what with our parents missing—stretching out ahead of us.

But not that Friday.

"I can't believe the Mr. McG gave us homework over the weekend!" Durinda complained. "Doesn't he realize some of us are too busy on Saturday preparing food for the Sunday feast?"

"The McG never gave us homework over the weekend," Georgia added.

It was true. None of our teachers at the Whistle Stop ever had, because the Whistle Stop had a no-homework-on-weekends policy. When Mommy was still here she'd explained to us that the school's theory was that if the teachers hadn't drilled enough into the students' heads between Monday and Friday, it was no one's fault but their own.

"This *Mr.* McG." Rebecca shook her head. "The man's got an attitude problem."

"I *know!*" Zinnia cried, for once agreeing with Rebecca. "Homework on the weekend—it's like the world's biggest anti-present!"

"And the way the Mr. McG assigned it." Petal shuddered.

"I know," Marcia said, proceeding to do a decent imitation of our new teacher as she quoted what he'd said. "'This weekend, be sure to study . . . *everything*.'" Marcia returned to using her own voice. "How is it possible for anyone to study everything?"

We didn't know. And here's a thing we hadn't known until just then: that Marcia could imitate a man's voice so well. Previously, the only one of us who could do that was Annie, who imitated Daddy's voice whenever she had to call Outsiders Who Didn't Know We Were Living Without Adult Supervision. But whenever Annie did it, she wound up using a British accent. Marcia's imitation of the Mr. McG had been perfect.

"Oh well." Annie sighed. "There's nothing else for it. Guess it's time for us to start studying everything."

"I wonder why he wants us to study everything?" Marcia wondered.

"Who knows?" Jackie said. "At least tomorrow is Saturday."

* * * * * * * *

The next morning, seven of us enjoyed the breakfast of chocolate chip pancakes that Durinda had prepared with Jackie's help in order to fortify us for the long day of studying ahead. We say seven of us because once again Marcia was nowhere to be seen.

"Do you think she's off again stealing your job of paying the bills?" Georgia asked Annie as Annie settled down with her schoolbooks. "And if so, would you like me to get the spear and threaten her with it to make her stop?"

The spear was part of the suit of armor we referred to as Daddy Sparky. We dressed him up in a quilted smoking jacket, corncob pipe, and fedora to throw off nosy parkers who peeked in our windows. We also had a dressmaker's dummy we referred to as Mommy Sally that wore a sleeveless purple dress, a string of pearls, and a wig.

Georgia was very fond of that spear.

"No, I don't," Annie answered Georgia. "All the bills for this month have been paid already, so unless Marcia's making up new bills just for the fun of it—"

"Oh, I forgot to mention." Durinda cut Annie off. "When Jackie and I were preparing the pancakes, Carl the talking refrigerator said that we were getting low on eggs and milk."

"How about pink frosting in a can?" Rebecca wanted to know. "Did Carl say anything about that?"

We ignored her. None of the rest of us cared quite so much about the pink-frosting situation as Rebecca did.

"I really do think," Durinda continued, "we'll need to do a big shop soon."

"Fine." Annie sighed as though the weight of the whole world were on her shoulders and her shoulders alone. She put aside the book she'd been trying to study. "I suppose I'll have to go up to the tower room now and get my me-imitating-Daddy disguise out of the costume trunk so that I can drive us into town to get more food."

That's when the telephone rang.

"Let's go see who's calling!" Zinnia urged, excited.

Since Mommy and Daddy's disappearance, we almost never answered the phone anymore, for a variety of very good reasons. But back in April, when we almost missed a call from the Tax Man, we'd realized that some calls were too important to miss. Since then, Annie had had caller ID installed so we could always tell who was calling us and decide whether we wanted to talk to them or not.

"I wonder if it's Will inviting us over to play!" Zinnia said as seven of us raced for the phone in the drawing room.

"I hope it's not Bill Collector!" Petal worried aloud.

"There's no one named *Bill Collector*," Georgia said with a Rebecca-worthy sneer. "There are people referred to as bill collectors, because that's the job they do, but there's no *Bill Collector*."

"Maybe it's the McG," Durinda said, "calling to tell us she's fired the Mr. McG."

"Has anyone else noticed," Jackie said, "that the McG has gone back to being as awful to us as she was before we rescued her from Crazy Serena? It's as though none of it ever happened!"

"I just hope it's not a telemarketer," Rebecca said. "I hate telemarketers. People trying to sell you stuff over the phone—how do I know I really want it if I can't actually see it?"

At last we were all gathered around the phone in the drawing room staring at the number displayed on caller ID.

Annie looked puzzled.

"Annie?" Durinda said soothingly. "What's wrong?"

"It's that number," Annie said.

"You recognize it?" Rebecca demanded.

"Yes," Annie said. "It's the number from the car phone. You know, the car phone inside our Hummer?"

"But what could it mean?" Georgia asked as the phone stopped ringing and then immediately started again, displaying the same number.

"*I* know what it means!" Petal said.

Six heads swerved in her direction, shocked. When did Petal ever know what anything meant?

"It's the ax murderer!" Petal shrieked as she started to run around in circles. "It's finally the ax murderer!"

"Petal," Rebecca said as Durinda and Jackie moved to put their arms around Petal and stop her circle running, "what *are* you talking about?"

"It's just like that ghost story they told us at camp the one time Mommy and Daddy sent us," Petal said.

"What story?" Annie asked.

"The one about the babysitter who keeps getting prank calls," Petal said, "the caller always asking, 'Have you checked the children?' But then the babysitter calls the police to have them trace the calls, and the police call back and say, 'Get the children and get out of the house—the calls are coming from *inside!*'"

The ringing stopped and started up again, same number displayed.

"This is *exactly* like that!" Petal said. "The danger is *inside* the house! The calls are coming from *inside* the house!"

"No, they're not," Rebecca said. "They're coming from the car."

"This is ridiculous," Annie said. "I'll get to the bottom of this." And then she picked up the phone, silencing the ringing.

"Hello?"

Unfortunately for the rest of us, since the only phone in our house that had speakerphone was in Mommy's private study and we were in the drawing room, all we could hear was Annie's end of the conversation.

"You're *where?* You did *what?*"

Pause while the other party talked.

Annie covered the receiver with her hand and addressed Jackie. "Run up to the tower room and check the costume trunk, see if my Daddy disguise is still there."

Jackie raced there and came back again—even when not using her power, Jackie was still faster than any of us—and shook her head.

"I can't believe you!" Annie yelled into the phone.

Another pause.

"Well, I suppose since you're already there . . . just a second." Annie covered the receiver again and turned to Durinda. "Do you have the grocery list ready?"

Durinda hurried from the room and returned a moment later with a list for Annie.

"Okay." Annie spoke into the phone again. "Let's see here . . . " And she proceeded to read the whole list, item by item. "All right then, I guess that's it," Annie said when she'd finished. "See you soon. Drive carefully."

Annie hung up the phone, looking as though she'd been thunderstruck by something big. Like a Hummer.

"Who was that?" Jackie asked.

"And why did you read my grocery list?" Durinda asked.

"It was Marcia," Annie said, dropping down into a wing chair.

"Marcia?" six of us shouted at once.

"Yes," Annie said. "Marcia. She said she got up earlier than the rest of us and was hungry. When she noticed we were low on supplies, she put on my Daddy disguise, grabbed the keys and the checkbook, and drove the Hummer into town. She was just calling from the parking lot to have me read her the list, to make sure she hadn't missed anything."

"Marcia?"

For the longest time, that was all any of us could think to say.

"Marcia?"

Because really, before that day, Annie had been the only one of us who knew how to drive. Or impersonate Daddy.

* * * * * * * *

"Marcia?"

We were still saying it an hour later when the subject of our wonder and confusion walked into the house wearing a man's suit, a false mustache, and a fedora, underneath which she'd stowed her two ponytails.

"Marcia!" we all cried.

"Isn't anyone going to help me carry in the groceries?" Marcia asked, wincing a little as she tore off her phony mustache. "It is an awful lot for one person to carry."

"Marcia." Annie's voice was cold as steel, and her face was turning purple with rage again.

"What is it?" Marcia asked.

"How could you?" Annie said.

"Yes," Petal said with rare force, "how could you? Annie's the only one of us who knows how to drive the car!"

"But it's so easy," Marcia said with a laugh.

"Easy?" Georgia echoed.

"Why, yes," Marcia said. "I've watched Annie do it a million times. Well, okay, maybe not a million, but enough. Why, anyone can drive a car—even Zinnia!"

(And here someone really does need to interrupt the story to say, *Hey, kids, don't try this at home!*)

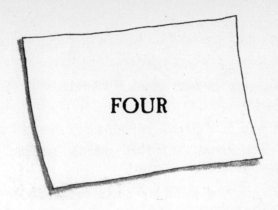

FOUR

The rest of the weekend passed uneventfully with us studying as the Mr. McG had directed, some of us studying more than others.

It was on Monday, as we bounced our way along to school in the little yellow school bus, that Marcia dropped her bombshell. As Zinnia might say, it was a doozy.

"I think," Marcia announced, "that we should have a vote to see which one of us should really be head of the family in our parents' absence."

"That's crazy talk," Rebecca scoffed.

"Annie's in charge," Jackie said.

"Always has been," Durinda said, "always will be."

Annie remained silent.

"But why?" Marcia asked. "Why is Annie in charge?"

"Because she's the oldest," Zinnia said simply. "It

may not be a fair system, but it's the way things have always worked in our family."

"Not only is that unfair," Marcia said, "it's also arbitrary."

"Simply put," Jackie explained to those of us who might not know, "*arbitrary* means 'random or by chance.'"

"Who do you think should be in charge instead of Annie?" Petal asked. "I hope you don't mean me—I'd hate having all that power!"

"Me," Marcia said. "I should be in charge."

"*You?*" Rebecca snorted. "You can't be. You're four minutes younger than Annie."

"And in our family," Georgia added, "four minutes is a very big deal!"

"Perhaps," Marcia said, "but Annie's mostly in charge because she can do things the rest of us can't, like pay the bills and impersonate Daddy and drive the Hummer. But now I can do all those things too."

Huh. We hadn't thought about that.

And here's something else we hadn't thought about.

From the very beginning of our troubles, if we'd been asked which Eight would be voted Most Likely to Stage a Coup, we would have guessed Georgia, with her spear obsession, or even Rebecca. But *Marcia?* Who ever paid attention to *Marcia?*

"And," Marcia added now, "we never did put it to a vote, you know, about who should be the boss of us ..."

Annie finally spoke. "Fine," she said. "Let's have a vote. Right here. Right now."

Six of us gasped. We'll leave you to guess which six.

"By a show of hands," Annie said, "how many of you favor Marcia taking over as head of the family?"

One hand went straight up: Marcia's.

"How many of you," Annie said, "favor me continuing as head?"

Six hands went up.

"Why didn't you vote?" Zinnia asked Annie.

"Because," Annie said, "I would never vote either for or against myself."

"I'm afraid Annie wins," Durinda said to Marcia soothingly. "But can't you see that it makes sense? After all, even if you can do all those other things, Annie's still the oldest and we're used to her being in charge. But more important than that, Annie's still the only one of us who can be as smart as an adult when needed. Annie's still the smartest."

Marcia didn't say another word as the little yellow school bus continued bouncing us on our way.

* * * * * * * *

The Mr. McG was waiting for us when we arrived at our classroom.

"Quick, put your things away," he said, hurrying us along. "Today is a very big day."

"What's going on today?" Mandy Stenko asked, her eyes darting to the right-hand side of the chalkboard, where we now all saw that only one word was listed under the schedule for the day:

Test.

"But the McG never sprang tests on us!" Rebecca objected, forgetting in her outrage that we only ever referred to our former teacher as the McG among ourselves or with trusted friends, never with People in Authority.

"Well," the Mr. McG said, "*Mrs. McGillicuddy* isn't your teacher anymore, is she?"

"Can we have a vote to get her back?" Petal asked.

The Mr. McG ignored her and continued, "It has come to my attention that your ... *previous teacher* was far too lenient on you. It is my opinion that you all need to be tested so that I can assess where you are in your education."

"What exactly is the test going to be on?" Will Simms asked as the Mr. McG gave a thick sheaf of papers to each of us.

"It's exactly as I told you when I warned you that you needed to study over the weekend," the Mr. McG said. "The test is on everything you've ever learned. *Everything.*"

Eight of us plus our classmates all gasped.

This was horrible!

We'd had evil substitute teachers (Crazy Serena); we'd had underhanded principals (Frank Freud); we'd even had teachers who were mean a lot of the time with no rhyme or reason (the McG). But we'd never been subjected to *this*. Here was an educator who actually expected us to *know things!*

And who among us knew everything, or even just everything he or she had ever learned? True, as a group we were smart enough that we'd skipped a grade early on, which explained why we were only seven and already nearing the end of third grade. Jackie was exceptional at reading and vocabulary. And Marcia was equally exceptional at math and science. (We won't talk about Petal.) But *everything?* Honestly, Annie was the only one of us who had a chance at knowing everything because she was the only one of us who could be as smart as an adult. Plus, she was the one who had spent the most time studying over the weekend.

With heavy sighs, we picked up our pencils and bent our heads to the test.

* * * * * * * *

"Annnnnd . . . *time!*" the Mr. McG called out. It seemed to us that it had been a week since we'd started taking the test, but a look at the clock on the wall revealed that only two hours had passed.

Still, a *two-hour test?* Our new teacher was evil!

Didn't he realize we were just little kids? We mean, it's not as though we were in college or anything.

"Please put down your pencils," the Mr. McG instructed, "and pass your test sheets to the front of the room."

When we'd done as he requested, he had another announcement to make.

"You may all take recess now," he said, "while I grade your papers. So enjoy your fun while you can." He paused, then added darkly, "And then we'll see what we shall see."

* * * * * * * *

Outside in the play yard, we tried to take our minds off our troubles by hanging upside down on the jungle gym, which was not easy to do. The hanging-upside-down part was easy enough, but taking our minds off our troubles? We shuddered every time we thought of that two-hour test.

"Did you see all those questions?" Zinnia asked.

"Yes," Petal said. "I was so busy counting how many

there were, over and over again, I forgot to answer most of them."

"What state is St. Louis the capital of?" Georgia asked.

"I'm pretty sure it's still Missouri," Mandy Stenko said.

"Oh dear," Georgia said. "But I put down New Orleans!"

"New Orleans isn't a *state!*" Rebecca said. "It's a country!"

"No, it's not." Will Simms corrected her, but in a nice way. "It's a city in Louisiana, but I for one can certainly see where Georgia would make such a mistake. See, both St. Louis and New Orleans are known for music— jazz, specifically—so even if the geography isn't quite the way Georgia imagines it, it should be."

We all paused to beam at Will. He was so good to us.

But then he spoiled it all by saying, "I really like our new teacher!"

"You *what?*" Jackie was shocked; in fact, a little outraged. She was always the most even-tempered among us, but even she couldn't possibly condone a teacher who sprang surprise two-hour tests on us!

"But I do," Will said. "It's kind of nice for me, after all these years, having another male in the classroom."

Huh. We had never thought of that: the idea that

there might be a loneliness factor for Will in being the only boy with nine other girls plus a female teacher.

Still, that was not a good enough reason for Rebecca.

"Honestly, Will," she said, for once disgusted with our favorite boy in the world. "If you want male companionship that badly, we could buy you a boy puppy!"

We continued to hang upside down from the jungle-gym bars, most of us not even noticing that the whole time we'd been out in the yard, Annie had said nothing about the test.

Neither had Marcia.

* * * * * * * *

The Mr. McG stood at the head of the classroom, our fate in his hands.

Okay, maybe we were being a little dramatic about it, but we did want to know how we had done on that test.

"This has all been very revealing," the Mr. McG said as he began handing back tests in an arbitrary manner. "Some of you aren't quite as smart as you probably think you are." He placed a test face-down on Mandy Stenko's desk and we heard her gasp in horror

as she turned it over. She'd gotten a big B- with an 83 next to it.

"Some of you did quite nicely indeed," he went on, placing a test on Jackie's desk. We couldn't see what it was but she looked happy when she turned it over.

"Some of you have peculiar minds." He placed a test on Rebecca's desk before moving on to Petal's. "While some of you . . . " He merely shook his head as he placed the graded test on her desk. Poor Petal. When she turned it over, she instantly burst into tears.

"As a group, you really could use quite a bit of work," he said, proceeding to place tests on the desks of Durinda, Georgia, Zinnia, and Will.

"In fact," he said, placing the final tests on the desks of Annie and Marcia, "only two of you did work that I would say was in any way superior."

Annie turned her paper over first and we could all see the big A+ with the 99 next to it.

Well, of course Annie had done the best. She was the one who'd studied the hardest, plus she was the smartest.

Then Marcia turned her paper over to reveal that her grade was an A+ as well, beside which was the only three-digit number any of us had scored:

100.

Marcia had received the highest score in the class.

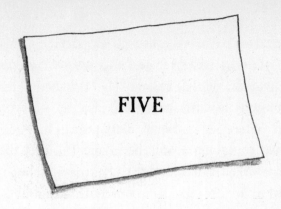

FIVE

Marcia waited until the little yellow school bus had deposited us back home and we were inside our house before requesting:

"A re-vote," she said. "In light of what happened today, I think we should have a re-vote to see which one of us should be head of the family."

Who would have suspected that one of our own might stage a hostile takeover?

"I'm just curious," Rebecca asked, "why this sudden grab for power?"

"There's nothing sudden about it," Marcia said. "The way things are around here—it's been bothering me ever since Annie made me switch rooms."

We knew what she was talking about.

Before our parents' disappearance, our sleeping arrangements had been the following: Annie, Durinda, Georgia, and Jackie—the four older Eights—in one bedroom, with Annie being the leader of that bedroom;

Marcia, Petal, Rebecca, and Zinnia—the four younger Eights—in the other bedroom, with Marcia being the leader of that bedroom. The two bedrooms were connected by a bathroom we all shared.

But after our parents' disappearance, Annie had switched things up a bit. She'd sent Durinda to be the leader of the bedroom with the three youngest and took Marcia into the bedroom with herself, Georgia, and Jackie, where Marcia was then the youngest. Annie's reasoning had been that since everything was so changed, Rebecca might torment Petal and Zinnia, and Durinda—being the second oldest of us all—was in a better position than Marcia to keep things under control.

Of course we'd been aware that this bothered Marcia, because she'd said so many times, but this much?

"And another thing," Marcia went on. "I don't particular like being the middle child. It stinks."

"But you're not the middle child," Georgia said. "There'd have to be an odd number of us for that to be true."

"Georgia's right," Jackie said. "You're not the middle. You're the fifth of eight."

"And you're the fourth," Marcia said to Jackie. "So we're both in the middle, the boring middle. I *hate* being one of the two middles, don't you, Jackie?"

Jackie looked puzzled by this. "No, not at all. I like who I am. I'm perfectly happy with my position in life."

"Ohhhh," Marcia said, "you're impossible."

"If you ask me," Rebecca said to Marcia, "your reasons are silly."

"Still," Durinda observed, "after what happened at school today, she does have a point . . . "

"Are we going to have a re-vote or aren't we?" Zinnia asked.

"Yes," Petal said, "I'd really like to know sooner rather than later if there are going to be changes around here because I have to go to the bathroom."

We all turned to Annie, who hadn't spoken yet.

"Fine," Annie said.

"Great!" Marcia said. "All those in favor of me taking over?"

Seven hands shot up.

"Well," Marcia said to Annie, "I guess I don't have to ask about votes for the opposition since we all know you never vote for or against yourself."

Just like that—so quickly!—big change had come to the Huit household.

"I'm sorry," Durinda said, placing a hand on Annie's shoulder. "But I'm sure you understand. If it were only that Marcia could pay the bills like you or impersonate

Daddy like you or drive the Hummer like you, it wouldn't be enough. But she *did* score higher than you on that test today."

"It's okay," Annie said bravely, brushing off Durinda's hand. "I do understand. And I'd have voted the same way you all did if I were the sort of person who ever votes against herself."

"Great," Rebecca said. "Now that we've all enjoyed a touching moment, will someone tell me what we're all supposed to do next?"

Instinctively, six heads turned to Annie. *She* always told us what to do when we got home from school. But as six of us looked at Annie expectantly, *she* looked over our heads to Marcia.

"Oh, right," Marcia said. "Durinda and Jackie, make us all a snack. Georgia, get the mail. Petal, go to the bathroom. Rebecca, try not to offend anyone for the next hour. Zinnia, feed the cats."

"Would you like me to get the spear for you?" Georgia offered.

"Yes, that would be nice," Marcia said.

"But what about Annie?" Georgia wanted to know after she'd returned with the spear and handed it over. "Aren't you going to tell her what to do?"

"I think Annie can figure something out on her own," Marcia said. "Besides, I have a headache all of a sudden. I think I need to lie down."

That was odd. Marcia had never complained of headaches before, nor had she ever had to lie down in the middle of the day.

And here's another thing that was odd. We looked over and saw Marcia's cat, Minx, blinking as though she'd been staring at the sun and then slouching down and covering her eyes with her tiny gray and white paws, little frown lines creasing her forehead.

Or maybe it wasn't so odd. After all, there were certain things—like getting our powers—that when they happened to us, they happened to our cats too. So maybe Minx was sharing Marcia's headache?

In any event, as we all hurried to do Marcia's bidding—particularly Petal—and Marcia slowly dragged herself up the stairs, spear in one hand, the other hand to her forehead, we all knew which bedroom Marcia was heading to.

The room where she could once again be oldest of the youngest.

There was a new sheriff in town.

* * * * * * * *

That week was a strange one for us. It was odd having Marcia in power. It was odd having Annie out of power. Who was Annie now? we all wondered.

And how, we wondered to ourselves but never out loud, would all this affect our chances of discovering what happened to our parents?

It was also a strange week because Marcia's management style was, well, *odd* after what we'd grown used to from Annie. Whereas Annie would give us directions and then keep half an eye on us to make sure her instructions were properly carried out, every time Marcia gave directions, she went to lie down, claiming to have a headache.

"Is all the power getting to you?" Rebecca asked snidely as Marcia dragged herself upstairs yet again, that spear looking heavy in her hand.

Marcia ignored her, muttering to herself something like "I wish those people in the Big City didn't have so many cars—they all whiz by so quickly."

Marcia had been muttering a lot of strange things like that, and Minx had been making pained meowing sounds and covering her eyes. We thought about asking Zinnia to talk to Minx and find out what was going on, but we didn't want anyone to think we were crazy.

And what was strangest of all about that odd week was that Mother's Day was coming up on Sunday. It would be the first Mother's Day of our lives with no Mommy around for us to celebrate.

What were we going to do?

* * * * * * * *

"Hullo, Eights!"

"Mr. Pete!" eight voices shouted.

It was late in the morning on Sunday, and we were all still in our pajamas because we were all depressed about its being Mother's Day with no Mommy or Daddy in sight. Then our doorbell had rung.

And there, in all his shining mechanic glory, stood Pete the mechanic.

"The missus and I were thinking, if you didn't have anything else to do today ... that is to say ... " For once, Pete looked nervous. Which was very odd, given that this was a man who could pretend he was our uncle and call himself Pete Huit at the drop of a hat and who could also wear an Armani jacket and run an evil relative out of town. Honestly, nothing ever ruffled Pete, other than one of us giving him a kiss on the cheek.

"If you were anyone besides Mr. Pete," Rebecca said, only semirudely, "I'd be telling you to spit it out right around now."

"Mrs. Pete and I just thought," Mr. Pete went on, "it being Mother's Day and all ... "

"You felt bad for us because we are orphans," Petal said.

"Well, no," Pete said. "I don't believe either of us put it quite like that."

"You want me to make Mother's Day dinner for Mrs. Pete!" Durinda said, looking flattered.

"Well, no," Pete said. "It would be rude of me to expect that. Besides, I made the dinner myself today, it being Mother's Day and all. In fact, I've got the whole meal already in the oven at home and I just need to pick up the cake."

"Mmm . . . *frosting.*" Rebecca's eyes flashed.

"I know!" Zinnia was practically jumping up and down, her bunny slippers flopping on her feet. "You want to invite *us* over to *your* house for the day!"

"Yes, yes!" Pete snapped his fingers. "That's the one!" Then he clapped his hands together. "Now, um, get dressed, get your things together, and then we'll be off." He looked embarrassed as he glanced at Annie. "Oops, sorry. I suppose that, being head of the family and all, you prefer to give directions under your own roof."

"Actually," Annie said with a calm that none of the rest of us could have mustered in her situation, "that's Marcia's job now."

Pete's eyebrows shot up nearly all the way to his hairline.

"*Marcia?*" he said.

* * * * * * * *

It was the worst Mother's Day of our lives because Mommy wasn't there, and neither was Daddy, and yet somehow the Petes made it better than it should have been under the circumstances.

After his initial shock, Pete said no more about the new power structure in our home, instead doing his best to make us feel at home in *his* home. Pete the mechanic, it turned out, made a mean lasagna, and by that we mean that it was good.

We all enjoyed playing with Old Felix, Mr. Pete's cat.

There was enough frosting on the Mother's Day cake for us to split it evenly, half the frosting for Rebecca, half for the rest of us.

And Mrs. Pete didn't even mind that we hadn't brought her any presents in honor of the day.

"I'm not a mother," Mrs. Pete said. "I'm just a woman who's lucky enough to have a husband who can make lasagna, plus, of course, I'm lucky enough to have all of you in my life."

We all huddled in to give her a hug.

Really, the only bad thing about the day—outside of the very big bad thing of missing our parents—was that poor Marcia was still getting those headaches.

"Huh," Pete said as Marcia massaged her temple with two fingers. "Maybe you should see a doctor about that? After all, you wouldn't want there to be anything wrong with your head."

* * * * * * * *

When we arrived home that night, stuffed and both happy and sad, Marcia headed upstairs immediately, not even bothering to grab the spear first, while the rest of us went off to the drawing room for some after-dinner juice boxes.

It was then that Jackie spotted the loose stone sticking out from the wall.

"That's odd," she said. "That only happens when there's a new note back there."

Durinda carefully removed the stone, and once it was out, we all looked inside.

There *was* a new note!

"Read it!" Petal shouted.

"Read it!" Zinnia shouted.

"I'll read it!" Georgia said.

"No, *I'll* read it!" Rebecca said.

"We'll *all* read it together," Annie instructed, since Marcia wasn't around to instruct us.

And so we did.

Dear Marcia,

Nine down, seven to go. This one does take some getting used to—hope you're feeling better soon!

As always, the note was unsigned.

But what could this possibly mean? The person—whoever the invisible, possibly magical person was—who left us these notes only did so when one of us received her power or her gift. With the occasional exceptions, like the very first note telling us the terms for discovering what happened to our parents and that insanely confusing one about *Beware the other Eights!* And only once had one of us received her gift before her power: the time Georgia sent her gift back.

So this could mean only one thing . . .

Seven Eights stood with hands on hips and shouted upstairs, "Marcia Huit, you get down here!"

And when she was down among us, groaning as she held her head, seven Eights glared at her and shouted:

"Did you perhaps get your power and neglect to tell anybody?"

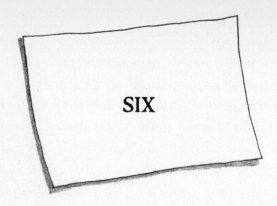

SIX

"Must you all shout so loud?" Marcia winced. "I already have a terrible headache."

"Of course we have to shout so loud," Georgia said. "We're outraged!"

"Yes," Marcia said, "but it's bad enough being me already. Oh, I *do* wish the people in the Big City would stop doing so many busy things. It's hard to keep track of it all. And all the lights in the room aren't helping my headache any!"

"Let's all go to Fall," Annie suggested calmly, naming the most peaceful of the four seasonal rooms Mommy had created for us.

"Good idea," Durinda said. "Fall is the most soothingly dark. You'd think Winter would be the darkest, but there's always so much glare from the snow."

So that's what we did: we went to Fall.

Petal immediately began making a big pile of fake

crinkly leaves so she could jump in them, which was fine with us. At least it kept her busy.

But poor Marcia was still groaning, as was Minx over in the corner. The other seven cats kept circling Minx quietly, their kitty brows furrowed in concern.

"Betty," Jackie instructed robot Betty, "do you think you might go into the kitchen and make Marcia a nice cup of tea?"

Betty rolled out of the room but it was anyone's guess if she'd do as instructed. More likely, she'd try to find cartoons on TV or flirt with Carl the talking refrigerator. Sometimes we did secretly wonder why, given what a great scientist Mommy was, so many of her inventions didn't seem to work quite as she'd intended them to.

But, miracle of miracles, robot Betty rolled back a few minutes later while we were all standing around Marcia wondering what to do. In Betty's pincered fingers she carried a cup of tea. It was a good thing that it turned out she hadn't bothered to heat the tea, because instead of placing it in Marcia's hand, she dumped it over Marcia's head.

"That's not helpful, Betty," Marcia said through gritted teeth, her twin ponytails and bangs now dripping.

"At least it stopped you groaning," Rebecca said.

"Maybe now you can tell us what your power is." Annie paused, an expression on her face that was different from what we'd seen the past few days. Ever since Marcia had staged her hostile takeover, Annie had seemed subdued, depressed even. But now there was a new light in her eyes, an intelligent curiosity. "And maybe you can also tell us," Annie added, that intelligent curiosity still there, "how long you've known you've had it."

"I don't know! You can't expect me to know the exact moment!" Marcia was outraged, and acting mighty suspicious. "You know how these power things are when you first get them. It's not always some kind of instantaneous thing like a light bulb going on over your head when you suddenly realize, 'Now I've got it!' Sometimes it's more gradual."

"Huh." Georgia looked dumbfounded. "My ability to turn invisible was pretty instantaneous."

"So was my ability to freeze people," Durinda said.

"Mine too," Jackie said. "One minute I was my regular self, and the next—poof!—I was faster than a speeding train. It's not the sort of thing a person fails to notice."

"Well, Annie's power didn't come upon her instantaneously," Marcia said defensively. "If I recall correctly, it was more of a gradual realization of what she could do."

"True," Annie said. "And now it's all gone, or at least the specialness of it is."

"But what is your power?" Zinnia asked Marcia eagerly. To Zinnia, getting powers was like getting presents. There was always a mixture of joy and sadness in her whenever someone received hers: joy at the idea of presents in general, sadness that she still had to wait until August for her turn.

"Oh!" Marcia grabbed her head again. "There goes the eight o'clock train!"

"I think I've figured out what Marcia's power is," Rebecca said knowingly.

"You have?" we all said as seven heads snapped in her direction, even Marcia's sore one.

"Yes," Rebecca said. "Marcia's obviously gone crazy. She's seeing things and hearing things that aren't here. So that's her power: the power to be insane."

We wouldn't have quite put it that way, but it did seem that Rebecca might have something there.

"Is that it?" Jackie placed a gentle hand on Marcia's shoulder. "You're seeing things and hearing things that aren't in the room with us?"

"Yes!" Marcia cried.

"You keep mentioning the Big City," Annie said. "Is

that where the things you're seeing and hearing are from, all the way over in the Big City?"

"Yes!" Marcia cried again.

"I think, then," Annie said, "your power must be that of superior hearing and vision, almost x-ray and telescopic vision. And what's more, you can't control the images and sounds bombarding you."

"Oh dear, this is serious," Durinda said as we all thought about what Marcia must be going through: the first of us Eights to get a power so overwhelming it could actually turn on her and cause her physical pain. "This calls for a cookie."

* * * * * * * *

Daddy Sparky and Mommy Sally kept us company in the dining room as we ate our soothing snack of chocolate chip cookies. Durinda had even dimmed the lights so that nothing would add to Marcia's headaches.

"Poor Marcia," Petal said, for once thinking of someone's worries other than her own.

"Poor Minx," Zinnia said. "If Marcia is in pain from all the images of the Big City bombarding her, what do you think Minx must be going through? I wonder what visions she's seeing ..."

"Why don't you ask her?" Rebecca suggested snidely, only to roll her eyes a moment later when Zinnia did.

We watched as Zinnia crouched down beside Minx and whispered in the cat's ear, then placed her own ear next to Minx's mouth so she could hear the cat's reply.

Zinnia patted Minx on the head before rising to her feet.

"Minx says," Zinnia said, "that there are too many dogs in the Big City. That if city dwellers had more cats than dogs, it wouldn't be so bad, but as it is now, it's just too much racket and barking and panting and seeing big dogs drool."

"Oh, brother," Georgia said.

"Minx further said," Zinnia further said, ignoring Georgia, "that if it weren't for the distraction of the headaches, she'd stage a hostile takeover of the kitty portion of our household just like Marcia did with the human portion. She says that Anthrax now lives in fear of this, the possible loss of power."

"My," Rebecca said to Zinnia, "Minx did manage to get an awful lot of words in, considering how short a time she was actually talking to you."

Almost any other Eight would have been offended by this, but Zinnia merely shrugged. "Sometimes it just works that way. Sometimes the cats say a little and I understand a lot."

"Oh no!" Petal said suddenly. "If Marcia can see all the way to the Big City, then that means she can see through walls. And if she can see through walls, surely seeing through clothes must not be a big challenge for her." She gasped. "Can you see my underwear?" Then she ran and hid behind a chair.

"No one can see your underwear," Durinda reassured her.

"And if they could," Rebecca said, "they wouldn't care."

"I think Marcia's power is awesome," Zinnia said admiringly.

"I do too," Annie admitted. "And I'll tell you something else."

We all turned to her.

"If we can just harness Marcia's power," Annie went on, "if we can just find a way to control it better, I'll bet we can really use it to our advantage."

* * * * * * * *

When we were younger and needed to solve something, Mommy would tell us to put on our "thinking caps." We suspected that she did this sometimes just to get us to be quiet for fifteen minutes so she could concentrate on whatever needed concentrating on at the moment. Still, we'd rather liked the idea of there really being thinking caps on our heads, and we pictured them looking like French berets in different colors. Annie's was always purple, Durinda's green, Georgia's gold, Jackie's red, and so forth, each Eight wearing her favorite color.

So that's what we did now. We all put on our thinking caps, trying to come up with a solution to the problem of Marcia's power being too big for her to bear.

"Try to block out the white noise," Durinda suggested.

"What's white noise?" Zinnia wanted to know.

"Is there such a thing as black noise?" Petal asked.

"White noise is too complicated to explain," Jackie said. "Think of it as too much static on the radio. It keeps you from properly hearing the song."

"Pretend," Annie advised Marcia, "that the world has shrunk down to the size of one thin dime."

"Or pretend," Rebecca said with a snort, taking off her invisible thinking cap and hurling it to the floor in disgust, "that none of us are acting like crazy lunatics. Honestly, Annie!" She snorted again. "Pretend the world has shrunk down to the size of one thin dime—like *that's* ever going to work."

"But it is!" Marcia sounded excited and not at all like she was bothered by a headache. "If I really concentrate my energies on just one spot in the Big City, I *can* block everything else out!"

Zinnia went over to Minx, bent down, and whispered in the cat's ear.

We saw Minx shrug her kitty shoulders as if to say *Why not? I've already tried everything else.* Then she squinted her kitty eyes, and a moment later, we swear, it was like a peaceful smile came over her face.

"One of these days," Georgia said to Zinnia, "I may just start believing you *can* do what you've been claiming all along."

"Don't worry," Rebecca said to Georgia. "If that day ever comes, I'll hit you over the head and knock some sense back into you."

"I think I've got it!" Marcia sounded even more excited now.

"What are you seeing?" Jackie asked.

"I'm seeing a woman in an apartment in the Big

City," Marcia said. "She's in her kitchen, and she's making liver and onions!"

"Eeeuw." Petal shuddered. "Can't you turn the world into one thin dime somewhere more pleasant?"

"I know where Marcia should focus her vision," Annie said.

"Where?" We all turned to Annie.

Annie went to stand behind Marcia. Then, placing her hands on either side of Marcia's face, she gently turned Marcia's head toward a particular direction.

"Try," Annie said to Marcia, "to see through this wall of our house and through the wall of our neighbor's house so you can tell us what's going on there."

Oh.

It was so perfect, it was beyond perfect.

Ever since the Wicket's return from her wild-goose chase in Beijing, we'd wanted to learn what she was up to. And now, perhaps, we would find out.

Marcia squinted her eyes at the wall.

"Concentrate, Marcia! Concentrate!" we all urged her.

"I can't," she said, "when you're all shouting at me so!"

We did our best to keep quiet, no one making a peep, except maybe Petal.

"I can see her! I can see her!" Marcia was excited again now.

But a moment later, excitement turned to terror.

"Oh no!" Marcia said, moving away from the wall.

"What is it? What is it?" we cried.

"The Wicket." Marcia gulped. "I just saw her. She was writing a note to Social Services. She said she was sure the eight little girls next door to her were living alone, without parental supervision." Marcia gulped again before adding:

"And she invited them to come investigate!"

SEVEN

"Cor, the Wicket's evil!" Georgia said, a mix of horror and admiration in her eyes.

"What does *cor* mean?" Zinnia asked.

"It's a British word," Jackie said. "It means something like 'gosh wow!'"

"Are we British, then?" Petal asked. "I have been curious about that."

"We might as well be," Rebecca said, "to hear Annie do her Daddy impersonation."

"If we're not," Durinda said, "I've been thinking of converting." She shrugged when we all looked at her. "It seems like it'd be fun."

"I'll tell you what's not fun," Annie said. "The Wicket turning us in to Social Services."

"Well," Marcia said, "at least I saw the Wicket *writing* to Social Services, not e-mailing or telephoning, so it should take her letter a few days to get there. And then who knows how many more days it will take them to respond? You know, bureaucratic red tape."

"Yes," Annie said, "but once they do respond, they'll probably send someone out right away to investigate and they'll discover that there are no adults living in our home. And then we'll all be split up, sent to live in different houses."

"Can't you just put on the Daddy disguise?" Zinnia suggested to Annie, but Annie just shook her head.

"What about you?" Petal said, her lip quivering as she addressed Marcia. "You *like* wearing the Daddy disguise now."

But Marcia shook her head too.

"That won't work," Annie said, "no matter who wears the disguise. The thing is, it may work when we're driving the car or when we're out in public. But it won't work at fooling anyone in our own home. For one thing, whoever comes to investigate will count the heads of those Eights not wearing the Daddy disguise and come up with only seven. Then the jig'll be up."

"Then what *will* work?" Rebecca demanded.

We looked at Annie. We looked at Marcia.

But neither had an answer.

* * * * * * * *

Monday we couldn't wait to get the school day over with.

Yes, yes, we did pay attention to the Mr. McG whenever we were in the classroom—that man! He was so obsessed with actually trying to teach us. And we maybe even learned a new thing or two, but we were still desperate to be done. We needed to get home so we could figure out what to do about the Wicket and Social Services.

"Cor blimey!" Georgia said to the bus driver on the way home. "Can't you drive this thing any faster, my good man?"

"No, I can't." The bus driver glared at Georgia in the rearview mirror. "It wouldn't be safe."

We all glared back at him but it did us no good. On that day, all the bounces on the little yellow bus were frustratingly slow bounces.

* * * * * * * *

Once again, we couldn't find Marcia.

Arriving home, we'd tossed our backpacks aside and raced through the snack that Durinda prepared for us with Jackie's help. Annie had said that for once we could put off doing our homework until later in the evening because we had more urgent matters than math and English to deal with at the moment: we needed to save ourselves. And to do that, we needed to brainstorm a plan.

So that's what we were doing. We were in the drawing room brainstorming a strategy to save our civilization as we knew it when we realized that one of our number was missing.

"Do you think she's gone out driving again?" Georgia wondered.

"Perhaps this time she's gone for a joy ride," Rebecca said. "I know that's what I'd do if I could drive."

"What's a joy ride?" Petal asked.

"It's exactly what it sounds like," Jackie said.

"Oh!" Petal looked pleasantly surprised. "It's so nice when words mean exactly what they sound like."

"Jackie," Zinnia said, "do you think maybe you should race up to the tower room to see if Annie's Daddy disguise is missing again?"

Jackie took off.

"Oh no! Did someone say 'missing'?" Petal's pleasure had turned to distress. "First Mommy and Daddy went missing. Now Marcia's gone too. Do you think we're slowly being picked off, one by one, by aliens who are transporting us in their spaceship to a distant planet where they will study us to see why we are the way we are?"

Rebecca studied Petal for a long moment before

speaking. "I must say, that's a very creative, if unusually long, delusion you're nursing today."

"I don't know what that means!" Petal said. "But what if I'm next? What if the aliens are taking me next?"

"You're not next," Rebecca said, growing bored.

"Well, technically, she is," Durinda said. "I mean, for getting her power and her gift. June is the next month."

"But I don't want to get my power and my gift next!" Petal said. "That's worse than being abducted by aliens!"

"Oh, bother." Georgia rolled her eyes.

And then Jackie was back, and she wasn't even out of breath.

"The Daddy disguise is where it should be," Jackie informed us. "And even though no one asked me to, I checked the garage. The Hummer hasn't been moved and the engine is still cool."

"My, you're getting slow," Rebecca said. "It took you all that time just to run up to the tower room, back down to the garage, and then here? And you used to be faster than a train!"

"I hate to say, Jackie," Zinnia said gently, "but that is kind of slow. For you, I mean."

"Well," Jackie said, not looking the slightest bit bothered by the insults, whether they were intentional or unintentional, "after checking the first two places, I did check every other room in the house, figuring she had to be here somewhere."

We thought about that—how many rooms there were in our house and how long it would take to thoroughly check all of them—and we realized that Jackie hadn't lost any speed at all. Well, not much.

"And?" Annie asked.

"And I found her," Jackie said. "She's in the basement."

"Not the basement!" Petal was horrified. To her, going into the basement was even worse than getting abducted by aliens.

"Yes, the basement. She's got on Mommy's old lab coat." Jackie paused. "And I think she's inventing something."

* * * * * * * *

Seven of us crept down the basement stairs, hoping to find out what Marcia was up to.

Despite Petal's fears, our basement was a rather nice place, certainly when compared with the Wicket's evil one. Our basement was where our scientist mother had created all of her greatest inventions.

Or at least the ones we knew about.

Unlike the Wicket's basement, with its coldness and

its barbed-wire fence around her wretched desk, our basement was warm and inviting. It even had orange shag wall-to-wall carpeting and a purple beanbag chair in the corner.

Funny, we thought, looking around and wondering why we never spent much time down there. It really wasn't such a bad place. There was hardly a spider in sight!

But then something else, bigger than a spider, came into sight.

There, behind Mommy's inventor's table, stood Marcia.

Marcia had on Mommy's lab coat, just like Jackie had informed us, but on Marcia, the hem of it fell somewhere around her ankles. Marcia also wore protective goggles over her eyes, and she was laughing—rather maniacally, it appeared to us—as she mixed potions in a test tube.

Beside her on the lab table were scattered wires and gears, all sorts of metal bits and pieces, plus an astonishing array of tools.

"You look like a mad scientist," Rebecca said.

"Thank you," Marcia said. She didn't glance up from her work, although she did look pleased, even if some of us suspected that Rebecca had *not* meant that as a compliment.

"Um, if you don't mind us asking," Annie said, "what are you doing?"

"I'm returning to our roots," Marcia said, measuring a little bit of this, stirring a little bit of that, and then pouring it all into a beaker and watching the liquid turn bright blue. "Mommy's an inventor-slash-scientist, so I'm simply following in her footsteps: coming up with an invention to save the day."

"But what is it?" Zinnia asked.

"It's a *device*." And now we could tell Marcia was concentrating very hard as her fingers flew among the scattered wires and gears, all sorts of metal bits and pieces, and the astonishing array of tools.

"We can see that," Georgia said. "But what sort of device?"

Marcia's hands were flying so fast—attaching this, twisting that, screwing on the other thing—her fingers might have been Jackie running!

"There!" Marcia stood back, pleased: somehow she'd managed to take every scattered item from the table and attach them all together to make one piece. Well, except for the beaker full of blue liquid. A moment later, Marcia looked up. She must have forgotten we were there until she'd sensed seven sets of eyes gazing back and forth from her to her invention.

"Oh, sorry," she said, looking embarrassed. "As I was about to say, my invention will save—"

"But aren't you going to add that blue stuff?" Petal interrupted. "It always gets me nervous when people make something from a kit and find pieces left over. Don't you think everything is there for a reason?"

"Oh." Marcia blushed. Then she shocked us by raising the beaker to her lips and taking a long slug right from it.

"You don't need that for your invention?" Zinnia asked.

"I hope you didn't just drink poison!" Petal gasped.

"Nope." Marcia wiped her blue mouth on her sleeve. "It's just my Kool-Aid for while I'm working." She passed the beaker around. "Anyone want some?"

Seven heads shook.

"Getting back to your invention and its purpose?" Annie prompted.

"Oh, right!" Marcia set down the beaker and picked up the device to demonstrate it. "Well, it's like this— you do this thing, that thing, and the other—like so. And then sound will come out of it. I found a video

"Let's try it!" we cried. Seven of us raced up to the drawing room as Marcia gathered together her device and her beaker of Kool-Aid.

Once we were all in the drawing room, there was some argument over who should be the first to talk into the device. At last it was agreed that Marcia should be. She'd invented the thing, after all.

So she went to the other room and Annie impersonated a Social Services type of person grilling us with questions, but all we heard back, first in Mommy's voice and then in Daddy's, was:

"Garble, garble, garble."

"Why isn't this working?" we heard Marcia cry in frustration from the other room. Then, after a heavy sigh: "I guess it's back to the drawing board."

"Oh, does that mean Marcia's invention doesn't work?" Petal wanted to know. "I thought *garble, garble, garble* was the sound of her drinking more Kool-Aid."

* * * * * * * *

But the drawing board yielded no better results on Tuesday; nor did the results improve on Wednesday.

And then Thursday came.

Since Marcia was now in charge, after Georgia collected the mail from the mailbox, she delivered it to Marcia instead of Annie.

"What's this?" Marcia said. There was just one long envelope. "Not another bill already!"

"Why don't you use your x-ray vision and find out?" Georgia suggested.

"Or quicker yet," Rebecca said, "look at the return address."

"Oh no!" Marcia held it up so we all could see.

In the upper left-hand corner, it said *Social Services*.

"They don't seem very social to me," Zinnia said.

"You'd better open it," Annie said, "so we know exactly what we're up against."

Marcia slit open the envelope and read.

```
Dear Blah-blah-blah,

This  is  to  inform  you  that  a
complaint  has  been  made  against
your household. Someone will be out
to investigate shortly.

Signed,
Blah-blah-blah
```

"I wonder how shortly is shortly?" Petal asked, looking around fearfully as though we might all be abducted to another planet any second.

"The Wicket just wrote her letter on Sunday," Jackie said.

"And this is only Thursday," Durinda said.

"Yet already," Georgia said, "we're hearing from Social Services."

"Who knew," Marcia said, "that the postal service could be so efficient?"

EIGHT

"I'll tell you one thing," Annie said.

We all turned to her.

"*Shortly* means shortly," Annie said, "even if we don't exactly know what *shortly* means to Social Services. We have to think quickly and come up with a new plan. We can no longer afford to wait for new inventions to decide to work properly. Why, look how long it's taken with robot Betty—and she's *still* not right!"

"So what should our plan be?" Georgia asked.

Six heads swung toward Marcia.

After all, she *had* wanted to be in charge.

Marcia looked at the device she'd invented. At various times since Monday, she'd taken half the gears and things out of it and reinserted them in different orders, but it still wasn't working. All she could get out of it was *garble, garble, garble.*

She shrugged, looking as sorry as a person could. "I got nothing."

As if watching a tennis game, six heads swung back toward Annie.

"I think," Annie said, "that what we need to do is call on Old Reliable."

"Old Reliable!" Rebecca snorted. "That sounds like the name of a horse!"

"No," Annie said. "Old Reliable is our mechanic."

* * * * * * * *

Some people when faced with trouble call in an expert. Other people when faced with trouble call in the Marines. But whenever we'd been faced with trouble, at least since our parents' disappearance back on New Year's Eve, we'd called in Pete the mechanic, from Pete's Repairs and Auto Wrecking.

Well, it worked for us.

"Hullo, Eights!" Pete said when we opened the front door that night.

For once, he wasn't arriving alone. At his side was Mrs. Pete. Nor was he arriving empty-handed, or armed only with his mechanic tools, although he had those, just in case. Rather, he and Mrs. Pete stood between two suitcases.

We invited Pete and Mrs. Pete in.

"Pete's told me about this place," Mrs. Pete said, her eyes wide with wonder as she looked around the front room, taking in the furniture, plus Daddy Sparky and Mommy Sally. "But mere words don't do it justice," she added as the flying watering can swooped down low, causing her to duck.

"I'll show you around," Durinda offered.

"I wish you would," Mrs. Pete said, going off with her and Jackie.

"Thank you for coming right away when we called," Annie said to Pete.

"Don't I always?" he said. It was the kind of thing that could have sounded smug or put-upon coming from anyone else, but from him it was merely a happy observation of fact.

"We wish we could tell you how long we'll need you," Georgia said.

"We hate to inconvenience you in any way," Rebecca added.

When it came to Pete, even Georgia and Rebecca didn't like to risk offending him. He was our golden goose, although we'd never seen him lay any eggs.

"Not to worry," Pete said in his easygoing way. "Emergencies take however long they take. You can't set a clock by them. So don't you worry, because I'm not worried."

"Lucky you," Petal said. "I'm worrying enough for all of us."

"What about Old Felix?" Zinnia asked, referring to Pete's cat. "You didn't leave him home alone, did you?"

"I could have," Pete said. "He's very self-sufficient. But no—whoops!—I forgot I brought him along."

Pete pulled his navy T-shirt away from his body and out popped the cat from underneath it.

Funny, you'd think a person would remember having brought a cat with him if that cat was under his shirt. Even funnier, we hadn't noticed Pete had a cat under there!

He really was an amazing man.

"Now, off with you." Pete gave Old Felix a gentle shove in the direction of the cat room, which was like our drawing room, only for cats. "Don't flirt too much with all the girl cats."

Just then Mrs. Pete returned with Durinda and Jackie.

"Oh!" she said to Pete as she clapped her hands together. "You should see the room they have for us to sleep in!"

"It's our parents' room," Annie said.

"You're too important to put in just a guest room," Zinnia said.

"But we did put fresh guest towels in the bathroom for you," Durinda said. "And pretty little soaps in the shape of seashells." Durinda reddened under Rebecca's glare. "I read somewhere that that's a nice thing to do for guests."

"I don't mean to rush anybody," Petal said, "but I am getting really worried here. Isn't it time we came up with a specific plan?"

"But shouldn't we all eat dinner first?" Mrs. Pete suggested gently. "I know I always think better with something in my tummy. Durinda, you didn't show me where the kitchen is. If you show me now, I can start supper."

* * * * * * * *

"What an *amazing* house this is!" Mrs. Pete said a half-hour later, laying aside her napkin on the dining room table. "When I asked you to show me where the kitchen is so I could start supper, I didn't mean start to *eat* supper—I meant start to *make* it."

"But it wouldn't be right," Annie said, "to expect guests to cook for us."

"Besides," Georgia said, "Durinda rarely gets to cook for anyone other than just us."

"She probably considered it a treat," Rebecca said. "What cook doesn't want to just keep doing it and doing it?"

"Well, it was very good," Pete said.

"It was only spaghetti and meatballs," Durinda said modestly.

"Well, I would love your meatball recipe," Mrs. Pete said. "Simply marvelous—and those shapes!"

"Um, that was a mistake," Durinda said. "They were supposed to be round. I honestly don't know how they turned into squares and triangles and rectangles."

Jackie leaned in close to Mrs. Pete and winked. "You should see what Durinda can do with a chicken."

We all laughed at that.

In fact, Durinda had never made us chicken, and we had no idea what she'd do with one.

We thought maybe she didn't like the idea of eating birds since she was so fond of the carrier pigeons— friends of Daddy—who occasionally brought us notes.

Funny, we hadn't seen a carrier pigeon in a long time, not since the day back in April when a flock of them all delivered the same message: *Beware the other Eights!*

But we didn't want to think about that. We didn't want to think about anything bad or dangerous in that moment, because for once we had adult company other than Daddy Sparky and Mommy Sally at dinner, and it felt good.

"I hate to say it ..." Pete said in a leading sort of way.

"You're right, of course." Annie sighed. "It's time we talk turkey."

Pete looked over at Marcia. "Well?" She continued gazing at her plate for the longest time before looking up and casting her eyes on Annie.

"Oh. I see." Pete gave out a low whistle. "So that's the way it is again. And that explains why Annie and not Marcia called me."

"Dessert in the drawing room?" Durinda said, breaking the tension. "Tonight I can offer you blue Kool-Aid and a choice of chocolate layer cake or pink frosting in the can."

* * * * * * * *

We were in the drawing room, each enjoying his or her dessert of choice.

Pete knocked back a slug of blue Kool-Aid before addressing Annie. "On the phone, you said you needed us both to come to your house to stay for an unspecified amount of time. It's not that the reason matters, but we are curious: why?"

"Our neighbor the Wicket notified Social Services about us," Annie said simply.

Both of the Petes looked horrified.

"My, my," Pete said. "She really is an evil toadstool, isn't she?"

"Yes," Petal agreed with a vehement nod of the head, "she really is."

"So we need you to pretend to be our parents," Annie said.

"I'm sorry to have to disappoint you, lamb," Pete said softly. "But I don't think we can do that."

"Why ever not?" Rebecca asked in a harsher tone than she usually used around Pete.

"Because we don't look a thing like you," Mrs. Pete answered with a sad smile.

"Fine," Annie said. "Then we'll say our parents are *both* in France this time, and that you're our aunt and uncle who are taking care of us."

"That could work," Pete said thoughtfully. "After all, I've pretended to be your uncle many a time. Pete Huit."

"That's right," Durinda said.

"We'll have to train ourselves to always call you Uncle Pete," Zinnia said.

"I think I'd like that," Petal said.

"So would I," Pete said with a wink.

"And what shall we call you?" Annie asked Mrs. Pete. "We don't even know your first name."

"It's Jill," Mrs. Pete said. "So I guess now I'm Aunt Jill."

"Aunt Jill." Annie tried it out. "That's good."

"And that makes you Jill Huit," Rebecca said, and then she laughed. "You know, it sounds funny if you run it together like that: Jillwheat."

None of the rest of us laughed. We didn't like to laugh at the people who were saving us.

"I guess the only thing left, then," Annie said, "is for us to tell you all about ourselves so that you can answer any questions the Social Services person asks you—you know, the sorts of things a regular uncle and aunt would know. And then quiz you on all of it."

"Only don't tell the Social Services person about our powers, Uncle Pete and Aunt Jill," Petal said with a shudder. "I don't think that will help matters any."

So that's what we did: informed and quizzed.

"You've been unusually quiet this evening." Pete turned to Marcia when we were finished and felt that they knew everything they needed to know about us, including the time Georgia got caught in an avalanche and enjoyed it. "Have you gotten your power yet this month?"

"Oh, yes!" Zinnia answered for Marcia. "And it's a doozy."

"She can see through walls," Durinda said.

"She can see all the way to the Big City!" Jackie said.

"Seeing through walls—it's how she learned what the Wicket had done," Georgia said.

"Her cat, Minx, can see through walls and all the way to the Big City too," Zinnia said.

"This house is simply amazing!" Mrs. Pete said.

"But don't worry," Petal reassured both Petes, "neither Marcia nor Minx can see your underwear."

* * * * * * * *

We wouldn't say that the next day, Friday, passed uneventfully. Rather, we would say it passed blissfully with our pretend relatives. Annie and Durinda had done their best these past months, but it was nice to have some adults around to tuck us in at night, kiss us on the foreheads, tell us everything would turn out okay.

But then Saturday came. Saturday, May 17. A glance at our calendar before going to bed the night before had informed us Saturday was Armed Forces Day ... whatever that meant.

And here, before we'd barely rubbed the sleep from our eyes, Marcia was racing through the house, shouting, "I see it! I see it!"

"You see what?" we all shouted, racing after her even though we had no idea what she was going on about.

"There's a car heading straight for our driveway and parking at the bottom of it!" Marcia yelled. "Now there's a man getting out of it and he's walking up the driveway toward our door!" she yelled louder. Then she paused before letting rip with the loudest yell of all:

"And on the pocket of his suit jacket, there's a badge that says *Social Services!*"

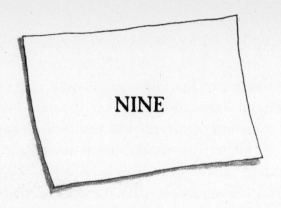

NINE

"What do we do? What do we do?" we all shouted.

"Quick, get dressed," Pete, who was thankfully already dressed, urged us.

We raced back upstairs.

That day as we dressed, we had the speed of Jackie. In fact, we changed so quickly that we were back downstairs when the doorbell rang, waiting all in a row, from oldest to youngest, like the family from *The Sound of Music*. Even the cats were lined up. Honestly, if we'd thought it would help our cause any, we'd have broken into song like that family from *The Sound of Music*. As it was, all we had to do was try to wait patiently as Pete opened the door.

"Hullo," he said good-naturedly. "Can I help you?"

We all craned our necks to see the man standing on our doorstep.

Huh. We'd expected someone from Social Services would look like the Face of Evil, but this man looked so ordinary. He was medium old, medium height, medium build, with medium short, medium brown hair and perfectly regular brown eyes. Really, the only thing not medium was his suit, which was on the rather raggedy and rumpled side. But perhaps he wasn't getting paid enough?

"I'm here from Social Services," he said, extending a hand for Pete to shake. "My name is—"

But before he could finish, we saw a flash of red, white, and beige coming at us from our neighbor's lawn. Suddenly, the Wicket was standing at the man's side. Who knew she could move so fast? She wore her usual outfit of red shirt with white polka dots and beige pants.

Toadstool.

She shook the hand that the man had been holding out toward Pete.

"Helena Wicket," she introduced herself. "I'm the one who wrote you about these . . . *children.*"

We didn't think anyone in the history of the world had ever invested the word *children* with quite so much venom.

"Yes, I recognize you," the Social Services man said, letting go of her hand as soon as was politely possible. "In addition to writing that letter, you also called us on the phone several times a day and came in person twice."

"Yes, well," the Wicket said, "I wanted to make sure someone got on the case in time. You know, I was just so worried about these poor abandoned ... *children.* That's why I came over now: I wanted to make sure you got the truth about these ... *children.*"

The man turned to Pete, held out his hand again.

"I was just about to introduce myself. I'm from Social Services." He paused. "My name is Bill Collector."

There was a crash from somewhere down the line of lined-up Eights.

Poor Petal had fainted.

* * * * * * * *

"Does that one do that often?" Bill Collector asked, indicating Petal, who was being fanned back into consciousness by Durinda and Jackie.

Petal was lying on the sofa in the drawing room, where we'd led Mr. Collector and the Wicket.

At least she hadn't brought a wretched fruitcake this time, we thought.

"Only every now and then," Mrs. Pete said. "Our Petal does have a bit of a nervous condition."

We thought that was a double nice touch: referring to her as "our Petal" and talking about Petal's condition as if she'd known us all her life. It made her sound like a real aunt.

"Sorry I have to ask this," Mr. Collector said to the Petes, "but who are you two? I can tell you're not the natural parents. You don't look a thing like these kids."

"I'm Pete Huit and this is my wife, Jill," Pete said. "We're the children's uncle and auntie."

"Auntie" was good too, we thought. Made it sound like we'd been related forever and not just since Thursday night.

"Nice place you have here," Mr. Collector said as he strolled around the drawing room, giving the suit of armor a tap with his pencil.

After the Petes had moved in, we'd taken the clothes off Daddy Sparky and Mommy Sally and returned Daddy Sparky to the drawing room and Mommy Sally to the upstairs. We'd figured that a dressed-up suit of armor and dressmaker's dummy wouldn't look right to nosy parkers once those nosy parkers were actually inside our house.

"Oh, all the decorating is my brother's doing," Pete said. "Robert's a model, you know, so he has great taste. As a matter of fact, that's where he is now, on an extended modeling trip to, er, *France*, and he took Lucy with him this time." Here Pete put a loving arm around Mrs. Pete's shoulders. "That's why we've come to stay with the kids. You know, until my brother and his wife come back."

"This man's last name isn't Huit!" the Wicket sputtered.

We were honestly surprised it had taken her so many minutes to say something awful.

"How do you know it's not?" Pete said cheerfully enough, as though the Wicket didn't scare him in the slightest. Well, we had seen him run Crazy Serena out of town. As far as we could tell, Pete was fearless.

"Because you're the town mechanic!" the Wicket cried. "Everyone knows who you are!"

"That's right," Pete said. "I am the town mechanic. I run Pete's Repairs and Auto Wrecking. My motto is If I Can't Fix It, I'll Wreck It for You. But have you ever seen a last name on anything to do with my business?"

The Wicket looked puzzled.

"No, of course not," Pete answered for her, "because there isn't any. Nor is there on my checks or my bills."

"You mean everything just says Pete?" Mr. Collector asked.

"Yes," Pete said. "I never have any trouble. They know me at the bank. They know me everywhere in this town. Besides, I'm the only Pete here, so it's not like anyone ever gets confused."

"But your last name is not Huit!" the Wicket insisted. "You are not Robert Huit's brother!"

"And why can't I be?" Pete said. "You think a mechanic can't be related to a model who lives in a stone mansion and has great taste? My, that's elitist of you."

"Elitist," Jackie whispered, "means the Wicket's a snob."

"Even if I'm not quite as trim or attractive as my model brother," Pete went on, "I clean up well enough."

"Well, even if I believe that you're who you say you are," Mr. Collector said in a tone that was agreeable enough, "I've still got to ask you some questions. The most important thing is that there are adults in this house supervising the kids and that they're being properly cared for."

"Ask anything you like," Mrs. Pete said. "We have nothing to hide."

"Let's see here . . ." Bill Collector pulled out the list. "The first thing to do is make sure that the children are healthy and well fed." He indicated Petal with his pencil. "Any health problems other than this one fainting?"

"Not a one," Pete said.

"How about food? Mind if I check your kitchen?" Before anyone could answer, he left the room. We heard him searching till he found the kitchen, then we heard the sound of the refrigerator door opening.

Thankfully, we'd had a word with Carl the talking refrigerator yesterday and told him not to say anything if any strangers opened his door. We'd also asked robot Betty to stay out of sight, and for once she was doing as asked.

"That's some well-stocked fridge," Bill Collector said, making a note on his list as he returned to the drawing room. "Looks like someone around here has done a big shop recently."

Out of the corners of our eyes, we glanced over at Marcia, grateful.

"Now then, you've got all that food," Mr. Collector said, "but who does the cooking?"

"I do," Mrs. Pete said. "Just last night I made spaghetti and meatballs. I shaped the meatballs like squares and rectangles and triangles."

"Interesting." Mr. Collector nodded his head appreciatively as he made another note on the pad. "I'd like to see the recipe that does that."

"Durinda?" Mrs. Pete said. "Could you get that recipe for Mr. Collector?"

In that moment, we loved Mrs. Pete a tremendous bunch. She was willing to lie if it meant saving us.

Durinda left the room and soon returned with the recipe.

"Are the girls going to school every day?" Bill Collector asked Pete.

"Oh, yes."

"Ever any problems in school requiring a parent?"

"I've been able to handle everything that's come up so far."

"Can you tell me a little bit about each girl?"

"Well, Annie tends to take charge; Durinda is very motherly; Georgia's been known to complain; Jackie's just an all-around great girl; Marcia has power issues when she's not busy observing things; Petal ... well, you already know about Petal. Rebecca can be rude, and Zinnia's always hoping for a present."

He *did* know us!

"Great stuff, great stuff," Mr. Collector said. He'd been busily taking notes all the while. "Now that that's settled, there's one other thing I'd like to ask you about."

"Yes?" Pete leaned forward.

"My car sometimes makes this pinging noise and—"

"That's it?" the Wicket shouted. "You're done asking questions and now you're going to have the man look at your car?"

"Well, what else is there?" Mr. Collector looked puzzled.

"Just because they say the ... *children* are healthy, well fed, regularly attending school, mostly behaving there, and they know one thing about each of the ... *children*, that's enough for you?"

Mr. Collector still looked puzzled. "What else is there?" he asked again.

"Can't you see they're lying?" the Wicket said. "These people," she said, pointing at Pete and then Mrs. Pete, "only just moved in here. I'm sure of it. I wrote you—and called and came in—because I'm worried about the ... *children*. It's not right for them to be here alone. They should all be moved to separate houses."

"But they have their aunt and uncle looking out for them," Mr. Collector said.

"And I keep telling you," the Wicket insisted, "these two aren't their aunt and uncle, and they *have* been living without adult supervision. As a matter of fact, I first wrote you because of what I saw."

"Which was?" Bill Collector prompted.

"I saw that one"—and here the Wicket's finger wavered uncertainly from one Eight to the next; she never could tell us apart—*"driving a car!"*

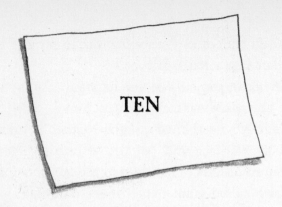

TEN

Oh, this was not good, not good at all.

The jig probably really was up now.

The Wicket had obviously seen Marcia driving the Hummer two weeks back.

"What exactly did you see?" Bill Collector asked.

"I saw that one." The Wicket's wavering finger still hadn't settled on any of us in particular. "She was wearing a ridiculous man's suit, a phony mustache, and an old-fashioned hat."

"Is this true?" Mr. Collector asked us gently.

In that moment, we all realized—even Petal—that there was nothing evil about this man. He was just an ordinary guy trying to do his job: keeping kids safe.

We opened our mouths to speak. We were about to admit the truth, that some of us had been driving.

But before we could say anything, Pete spoke.

"I think I can explain all this," he said, then he disappeared from the room.

We all waited in silence for him to return.

It felt like a long wait.

When he came back in, he had on the Armani jacket and wide tie we'd seen on him at other times. On his head was the fedora, and beneath his nose was the phony mustache.

"You mean this?" Pete said to the Wicket. "I had on my Halloween disguise."

"In *May?*" the Wicket said.

"Yes," Pete said. "It's never too early to try out a Halloween disguise on the public, see how it goes over, so you know whether it's the right one for you or not."

"What're you supposed to be?" Bill Collector asked. "Myself, I never can decide what to go as on Halloween."

"I call this costume Man with a Mustache," Pete said proudly. "Do you like it?"

"Oh, yes," Bill Collector said. "Very convincing."

"But it's not convincing at all!" the Wicket shouted. "I know what I saw!" she went on. "And it was not a big person like that driving—it was a little person, like one of those!" She pointed waveringly at all of us once again.

Pete hunched over so that it looked like his body had shrunk in size, then he put out his hands as though he was holding on to an imaginary steering wheel. "Is this more like what the person you saw looked like? See, I forgot to mention, I was also trying out an alternative costume, Short Man with a Mustache."

"Oh, that's a good costume too," Bill Collector said appreciatively. "I think I may like that one even better."

"But-but-but," the Wicket sputtered.

"Gently said," Bill Collector said to her, "you, my dear, need to get your eyes examined. And you need to stop bothering this family."

With a *harrumph*, she marched out, and Bill Collector turned once again to Pete. "Now, about my car . . ."

The two men headed toward the front door.

The whole time Bill Collector had been there, from start to finish, we'd hardly said or done a thing, save for Petal fainting and Jackie telling us what *elitist* meant. For once, we'd realized that it was probably safest to let others do the talking for us.

And now we were safe, safe from being split up from one another—at least for the time being.

"Hurray for Aunt Jill!" we said, circling around her for a hug.

And when Pete returned from helping out Bill Collector, we hurrahed and circled and hugged him too.

* * * * * * *

We enjoyed a celebration brunch with the Petes, and then they packed up their suitcases. Now that the most recent emergency had been handled, it was time for them to head home.

"We'd love to stay on," Pete said, "but Old Felix is finding it a bit much."

"He just gets confused by all this space you have here," Mrs. Pete added.

"But the offer we made back in February still stands," Pete said.

"Yes," Mrs. Pete added. "You're welcome to come stay with us until your . . . *situation* resolves itself."

"It's not that we're not grateful," Durinda said.

"It's just that we feel we have to go it alone," Annie said.

"Well, except for times like today, with Bill Collector, when we really do need help," Jackie corrected.

There was a tiny gasp.

Poor Petal. As nice as the man had turned out to be, anytime anyone said *Bill Collector*, Petal gasped, experiencing the horror anew.

"I understand," Pete said. "Just be sure to call whenever you need us for anything."

"Oh, I do love this house!" Mrs. Pete said, giving one last look around her. "I particularly love the seasonal rooms. I swear, I think I got a tan in Summer!"

We looked at her; she did look browner.

They stepped out the door but then Pete turned back.

"You're going to have to start talking again one of these days," he said to Marcia. He gave her a light chuck under the chin and her eyes met his. "Things'll get better for you. Chin up, lamb."

And then they were gone.

* * * * * * * *

"It seems to me," Annie said to Marcia as soon as we'd shut the door behind the Petes, "that now would be a good time for you to start talking."

"About what?" Marcia said nervously.

"Your power," Rebecca said snidely.

Rebecca may have been the one who said it snidely, but it had been on all our minds.

"What about my power?" Marcia asked, more nervous yet.

"How long have you had it?" Petal asked.

"I can't imagine getting a power," Zinnia said, "and not telling everyone else about it right away. I'd be so happy that I'd want to tell the world."

"You see," Jackie said gently, "we all know you had to have received it sometime before we found the note behind the loose stone."

"But what we don't know," Durinda added, "is how long before."

"Er, a while?" Marcia asked as much as answered, twisting her fingers as she did so.

"*How long?*" Georgia insisted.

"Since right before the Mr. McG handed out the big test?" Marcia asked-answered again, still twisting her fingers.

We all stared at her as the truth dawned on us.

"You got your power, your power of x-ray and telescopic vision, before the test," Annie said in a voice empty of all emotion.

"Yes?" Marcia asked-answered.

"And did you use it to see the test answers on the Mr. McG's answer key?"

"Yes?" Marcia asked-answered.

So *that's* how she'd outscored Annie!

In a way, this made us feel good. Our universe, as confusing as it often was, had tilted back to what we'd come to think of as normal. It was fine for others of us to be smart, to be as smart as we could be, but none of us could be smarter than Annie. In the absence of our parents, we needed to have one of us take the reins.

But it also made us feel bad, because it meant that one of us was that thing no one should ever be: a cheater.

There was no anger or resentment in Annie's voice, only a deep sadness, as she said what the rest of us were thinking:

"Oh, *Marcia*."

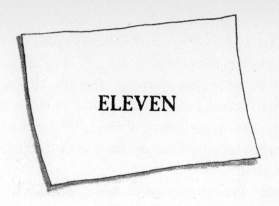

ELEVEN

Monday morning, before the Mr. McG had even had a chance to begin roll call—a practice we always thought was very odd, since with only ten of us in the class, it was obvious who was there and who wasn't—Marcia raised her hand.

"Yes, Marcia?" the Mr. McG said.

"I have a confession to make," Marcia said, "and I need to make it to you and the entire class."

At home, we'd talked about the difference between the lies we'd told to save ourselves—like saying the Petes were our aunt and uncle—and cheating. We'd concluded that cheating was wrong, no matter what the reason, and that Marcia would have to tell the Mr. McG what she had done.

But none of us had ever imagined she'd confess in front of the whole class.

"And what do you have to confess?" the Mr. McG asked now.

"That test you gave us?" Marcia said. "You know, the test about *everything?*"

"I well remember giving it," the Mr. McG said.

"Well," Marcia said, "I did know a lot of the answers already. I even knew most of them." She paused before continuing bravely, "But on the ones I didn't know, I, um, cheated."

There were two gasps in the room then, one from Will Simms and one from Mandy Stenko. Well, the rest of us had no reason to gasp. We Eights already knew about it, and the Mr. McG just wasn't the gasping type.

"Oh!" Mandy said. "That's practically criminal. You'll probably get expelled for that."

Leave it to Mandy to immediately leap to the worst possible outcome for this. But of course it's what we all feared: that Marcia would get expelled.

"But that's not possible," the Mr. McG said.

"Oh, I'm fairly certain it is," Mandy said. "I've read the student-conduct handbook backward and forward, many times. You could even say I've memorized it. And it specifically says on page seventeen, paragraph two, in the third sentence—"

"I didn't mean that," the Mr. McG said, cutting her off. "I meant that it's impossible for Marcia to have cheated. I had the answers locked in a drawer, and I keep the key to it on me at all times."

"But it is possible," Marcia said quietly, not looking away from his questioning gaze. "I did cheat. I was able to *see* the answers."

The Mr. McG stared at her for a long moment and then he let out a low whistle. "Oh. I see. Mrs. McGillicuddy—my wife; your principal—did tell me a few . . . *things* about you Eights, something vague about your parents and something about Georgia being able to make herself invisible, but I thought she was just talking crazy talk, as she sometimes does."

"You mean one of you used your powers for personal gain?" Mandy was outraged.

"Shh!" Will tried to quiet her. "No one else is supposed to know about their—"

"It's okay, Will." The Mr. McG stopped him. "It appears that everyone, at least inside this classroom, knows all about the special talents of the Eights now."

"I suppose you have to expel me," Marcia said with a brave sadness.

"That all depends," the Mr. McG said. "Of course, I'll have to throw out your perfect grade and retest you. If I do that, will you promise not to cheat?"

Hope entered Marcia's eyes as she answered, and we don't mean asked-answered, "Yes!"

"But what about the future?" the Mr. McG wanted to know. "How can I be sure you won't cheat again?"

"Because I give you my solemn vow not to," Marcia

said solemnly. Then she smiled. "Anyway, as of Sunday, June first—less than two weeks away!—my, um, *ability* will disappear. Well, sort of. At least, it will go into hiding. Only Annie's outlasts her month consistently, and that's because hers is just natural. Oh, and Jackie's still fast, just not like a train."

The Mr. McG shook his head, as though trying to remove nonsense out of one ear that someone had poured into the other.

"Sounds good enough to me," he said at last. "I'll retest you tomorrow morning. And be sure to study." He tossed a piece of chalk in the air with one hand, caught it behind his back with the other. Perhaps he wanted us to see that he had hidden talents too? "Okay, class, open your notebooks. Today we're going to begin our study of Japan, focusing first on the rise of anime."

We opened our notebooks and sat back in our seats, feeling vastly relieved. Marcia wasn't going to be expelled!

We realized then that, just like with Bill Collector, maybe the Mr. McG wasn't as evil as we'd suspected him of being. *Maybe* he just wanted us to learn things. Why, under his guidance, we could practically feel our brains *growing!*

In honor of our newfound positive feelings for the Mr. McG, we all spent the rest of the week studying really hard.

Finally, we'd found an educator we could respect.

* * * * * * * *

The following Monday was Memorial Day.

It was a somewhat sad time for us. It being a day of remembrance, we were remembering and missing our parents.

We were lounging around the drawing room, since we had the day off from school, feeling rather sorry for ourselves. All except for Marcia, who was again nowhere to be seen.

Then, into the silence, came two achingly familiar voices that we hadn't heard in a very long time.

"Annie, I love you," Mommy's voice said.

"Annie, I love you," Daddy's voice said.

As we sat there in shock and awe, we heard Mommy's and Daddy's voices say the same thing to each of us in turn, except Marcia.

"Where is that coming from?" Zinnia asked.

"If those turn out to be ghosts, I will be scared," Petal said. Then she smiled. "But it is nice, being told that I am loved."

"Marcia Huit!" Annie bellowed. "Get in here!"

A moment later, Marcia was with us, red-faced.

"You finally got your invention to work, didn't you?" Annie asked severely.

"Yes," Marcia said nervously. "I thought everyone would like it, but maybe I miscalculated?"

"Like it?" Annie thundered. Then a huge smile broke across her face. "Are you kidding me? I don't like it. I *love* it."

"It was practically the best present ever," Zinnia said.

"I have to admit," Rebecca said, rubbing her eyes with her sleeve impatiently, "even I got a tear in my eye."

"Oh!" Marcia looked relieved. "I'm so glad!" Then she got more serious. "Annie, I've been meaning to tell you . . ."

"Yes?" Annie said.

Marcia took a deep breath. "I hereby formally return the leadership of the family to you."

Rebecca snorted. "That's a laugh! I'm pretty sure we all knew that *that* had already happened."

Apparently, Rebecca had already recovered from feeling sentimental.

"Thank you," Annie said to Marcia without sarcasm, as though Marcia had had some choice in the matter. "But I'm curious. Why the need to make a formal transfer of power now?"

"Because I thought about it," Marcia said, "and I realized I don't deserve to be in charge. It was too much for me. I guess I just realized that I don't have an original idea in my head, not when it comes to leadership. I'm only good at following the blueprints of others."

"Are you kidding me?" Georgia said, sounding genuinely surprised. "But you thought up that amazing device from which we can hear Mommy's and Daddy's voices!"

"But it didn't work when we needed it most," Marcia said.

"So what?" Even Rebecca had to admit it worked just dandy now.

"And it is lovely," Durinda said, "hearing them again."

"Yes," Marcia said. "But it was Annie who saved the day. It's not even her month, and yet she came up with the brilliant plan of calling in the Petes."

"Who cares who came up with what or whose power was used?" Zinnia said.

"Exactly," Petal said. "I'm just glad we were saved."

"But it was Annie's power saving us again," Marcia said. "As for my power—*ha!* A fine power it turned out to be! All it did was nearly get me expelled."

"Are you kidding me?" Annie said. "It was your power that enabled you to see the Wicket writing that letter to Social Services. It was your power that enabled you to see Bill Collector arriving at our house so early. Honestly, Marcia, if it weren't for you and your power, we'd never have known of the coming danger in the first place. If it weren't for you, nothing I did could have saved us."

A slow smile spread across Marcia's face. "I really did do all that, didn't I?"

"Yes, yes." Rebecca yawned without bothering to cover her mouth.

"Shall we have lunch?" Durinda suggested.

* * * * * * * *

After lunch, we decided to spend some time outdoors working in our garden.

"I'm parched," Durinda said, wiping her wrist across her forehead after we'd been digging in the dirt for a few hours.

"No one our age says *parched*," Rebecca said.

"I don't care what anyone else says," Durinda said. "Would anyone like some lemonade?"

Whether any of us would ever use the word *parched* no matter how old we got, lemonade did sound good right around then.

We followed Durinda into the house and even helped cut up the lemons. But when we went to the dining room to drink it, we saw that something had been draped over the back of Marcia's chair.

"That must be your gift!" Zinnia cried.

Marcia lifted it carefully from the chair's back and held it up for all to see.

"Ooh, I see your favorite color must be purple too!" Durinda said.

"It's a cloak," Georgia said, adding, "I think."

"What's a cloak?" Petal asked.

"It's a loose outer garment," Jackie said, "so it's

of Mommy and Daddy's wedding, then I took their recorded voices off that, inserted the sounds into this, and then somehow programmed the thing so we can speak into it over here but whatever we say will come out in the drawing room or the living room sounding exactly like Mommy or Daddy."

"That sounds . . . involved," Rebecca said, for once too stunned to be snide. She was that in awe of Marcia's intelligence. We all were. This really did seem like rocket science to us!

"But who will talk into it?" Annie asked. "And won't the Social Services person notice if there are only seven of us in the room? Remember, that was a problem with the idea of one of us wearing the Daddy disguise."

"Oh, that." Marcia pooh-poohed her concerns. "When anyone asks, we always say that one of our parents is in the bathroom with a tummy virus and the other is in France. Well, this time we'll say they both have tummy viruses and that it might be contagious, which is why they can only talk but not be seen. Then we'll each take turns excusing ourselves, go to the other room where the device will be hidden, and impersonate Mommy and Daddy through the device. And voilà!" Marcia wiped one hand against the other. "Problem solved!"

Well, it didn't sound quite that easy, but since we didn't have anything better, or even anything else . . .

neither a coat nor a cape but something sort of in between."

"It looks like it would be great for concealing things," Rebecca said. As Marcia tried it on, she added, "If it were only dark and plaid, you'd look just like Sherlock Holmes. Maybe we need to get you a funny hat."

"Now you see?" Annie said to Marcia. "We're not the only ones who think you and your power helped us out a lot this month. Obviously, whoever leaves these items for us thinks you're worthy of a gift too."

"Thanks." Marcia beamed at Annie.

And we could see that, at least in that moment, Marcia was pleased with her station in life, perfectly content to be who she was.

"Ooh!" Zinnia cried. "If Marcia got her gift, there must be a new note!"

When we raced into the drawing room, we saw that Zinnia was right. Since it was Marcia's month, it was her privilege to remove the stone and read aloud the note that had been left for her there.

Dear Marcia,

Ten down, six to go—splendid! And as you can tell, I still have those stellar math skills you always comment on! Let's

see, though. If the first five of you have
knocked the first ten items off the list,
which of you will have to knock off the
eleventh and twelfth?

And that was it. As always, the note was
unsigned.

But we did think long and hard about that last line
of the note, and then seven heads slowly swiveled in
Petal's direction.

Oh no.

Petal was next.

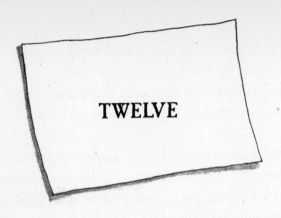

TWELVE

The next day we were back in school again, still pleased with our new teacher. And that afternoon, we were back home again, pleased with just about everything.

We were mostly pleased that the end of May was now in sight.

"I'm just glad that the madness of this month is nearly over with," Georgia said.

"Yes," Rebecca said darkly, "but I fear next month will be even worse."

"I hope June never comes!" Petal said.

Was there ever an Eight who wanted her power less, even though it meant getting a gift too?

Still, we were all glad to have May nearly over with, glad we'd avoided possible disaster with Social Services.

True, we still had many questions hanging over our heads. We could almost picture them up there, millions of tiny question marks, twinkling like stars in the night.

Okay, maybe not millions, but enough.

And so many of those questions didn't even have hints of answers yet, wouldn't have until August.

But for now, it was enough that we had one another, that we were still together, and that we were back to the state of what passed for normal in our world.

"Okay." Annie clapped her hands together. "The end of the school year may be in just a few weeks, but we all still have to do homework until then. Petal, you shut off the TV. Zinnia, you feed the cats. Durinda, you make us a snack. Jackie, Marcia, Rebecca, you get the homework sheets out of the backpacks. And, Georgia, you go get the mail. We haven't had any since Saturday, what with the holiday weekend, and there should be some bills in there. I do *not* want to be late paying the bills."

"That would be awful." Petal shuddered. "I wouldn't like to have Bill Collector come back, even if he did seem awfully nice for someone with the power to split us all up."

We didn't bother correcting Petal and telling her that Bill Collector came from Social Services while bill collectors would come from somewhere else. There were only so many times we could repeat ourselves.

Georgia returned with an unusually large stack of mail, which she happily dropped in front of Annie. From the beginning of our troubles, Georgia had always seemed happy to drop a lot of mail in front of Annie.

"Bills, bills, and more bills," Annie grumbled, but there was something false to that grumble and we had the feeling that after Marcia's grab for power, Annie was rather pleased to see bills if it meant she was the only one who could pay them.

"Hello! What's this?" Annie said, holding up an envelope.

"Looks like a cream-colored envelope to me," Marcia observed.

"Have bill collectors started getting fancy?" Rebecca wondered, not sounding terribly interested in the whole thing.

"It looks like some sort of invitation," Durinda said.

"Ooh!" Zinnia said. "I hope we've been invited to a party!" Then her face fell. "But whose party could we possibly be invited to?"

"That's right," Georgia said. "Will's birthday party was in January and Mandy's won't be until December."

"We haven't sent ourselves an invitation to our own birthday party in August," Petal said with a puzzled frown, "have we?"

We ignored Petal. We knew that soon enough—all too soon!—we'd be required to pay lots of attention to her.

"It definitely is an invitation to something," Jackie said. "See the pretty slanted handwriting? That's called calligraphy."

"And look," Annie said. "It's addressed to 'Robert and Lucy Huit and the Eights.'"

"Open it!" seven Eights cried at Annie. "Read what it says!"

And Annie did.

You are cordially invited

to

the wedding of

Martha Huit

&

George Smith

on Saturday, the 21st of June, 2008,

in France.

Hold on a second here.

We were being invited to a *wedding?* In *France?*

And who, by the way, were Martha Huit and George Smith?